Promise of the Good Luck Coin

BY JERRY W. DEAN

Jerry W Dean

12/28/20

To an Old Friend & fellow Viet Nam Vet!

DORRANCE
PUBLISHING CO
EST. 1920
PITTSBURGH, PENNSYLVANIA 15238

Prologue:

This is a story that spans time, from the depression to the Vietnam Era. A story of forbidden love, a story about an old good luck coin that saves lives and brought forth a new one. A story of a child that grows up, his joys, his struggles and his search.

70% non-fiction 30% fiction

Acknowledgments:

I want to thank the following for their support and assistance in producing this story.

My wife Wanda, Sarah Buday for typing, Abbey Few for typing, Karen Honeycut for editing, and Paul Heidepriem for photographic copy work.

Many names of people who have passed on were written into this story, people that I knew. This will, in a small way, immortalize their names.

ARCHIE GREW UP ON A FARM in rural North Carolina, in a community named Berea. He was born in 1919, the oldest of three children. His sister, four years younger, was Marilee, and the youngest was brother Brindell. Archie's full name was Archie Allen Wilkins. Their parents were Willie "Lee" and Mary Bowling Wilkins.

They all worked hard on the farm growing tobacco, corn, wheat, hogs, cows, and chickens. Farm life is sustained by what was grown there. Cows provide milk for drinking and meat to eat as did hogs and chickens. Chickens also supplied much needed eggs for breakfast and a necessary ingredient for desserts. They had horses to pull the wagons loaded with their crops, wood to burn for heat, and plows to turn the soil. The two horses were sometimes used for transportation to school, visiting neighbors, and cowboy and Indian chases.

By 1929 there were school buses in rural areas; prior to that, the children walked or rode mules or horses to school. Even after the buses, often they still had to walk or ride their horses or mules because of road conditions. The roads were dirt, poorly maintained, and there was little money for gravel. The Great Depression had begun. During the heavy rains, roads were not passable by vehicle. In order to get an education, they had to revert back to walking or riding their mules or horses. Sometimes, when the roads were not passable in the mornings, they would be in the afternoon if there had been a lot of wind and or sunshine.

There was a shed there at school called the horse and mule shed. This was used for years to shelter the animals while their riders were in school. There were watering troughs for the animals and always hay for them to eat. After the school busses were provided by the county, the building was then called the bus shed but animals were still kept there as needed.

When Brindell started to school, he would ride double with Archie. This was necessary because he was at risk of falling off. Archie always did his best to hold Brindell on Old John, their most beloved horse. Brindell's legs just weren't long enough to wrap over the back of the horse and grip him. He did occasionally fall off without getting hurt; mud is soft. You could just look at him and see that he had fallen off due to the mud caked on him. Marilee rode another horse and never fell off. Old John was a gentle horse, and the children said he had a sense of humor because he snickered when anyone did fail off. He was so gentle that Brindell would sometimes pull up on his tail when trying to mount him.

On the occasion that the animals were ridden to school in the morning and the buses were able to travel in the afternoon, the children would ride in the back of the bus with the rear door open holding the reins and leading the animals. The bus had to drive slow due to road conditions and the animals being led. Old John insisted on walking with his head inside the rear door where he was admired by all. Fortunately, home was only three and one half miles from school.

Archie was a hunter, and there were many turkeys, squirrels, and deer brought to the kitchen table by his skill. Two of his friends, Nat Daniel and Stanley Brooks tried hunting with him but had little luck. He always seemed to be the one that had success. He was respected by friends his age and adults. He had quite the reputation and some called him "The Sharpshooter." He always had stories to tell about stalking and making the kill shot. Archie had discovered something no one else knew about at the time. One day, while he was deer hunting, a deer was running through the woods too fast for him to take a shot. For the heck of it and to expel his frustration, he whistled loudly. The deer immediately stopped running and stood there looking around. That's when Archie shot him. He was so inspired that this worked, he started experimenting. He found that sometimes when deer or turkeys were in a thicket or brush, if you started whistling in low tones, they would come out of hiding to investigate.

Archie didn't tell others about what he discovered; he just kept amazing everyone with his hunting skills. Many years later when regaling his Army buddies about this technique, one asked what he whistled in these low tones. He said it was his mother's favorite hymn, *Amazing Grace*. Archie graduated from high school in 1937 and his reputation as a hunter grew each year. He worked hard on the farm with the rest of the family. Sunday was their day of rest and worship at church where his mother, Mary, sang in the choir.

He was indeed a fisherman too. Approximately one and a half miles from the house was a grist mill on Tar River. His daddy, Lee, would travel there, wagon loaded with corn or wheat to have ground into cornmeal and flour. The mill pond was large with a dam that Archie loved to fish from. Each time Lee went to the mill, Archie tagged along with his fishing pole. The story goes that on one of these trips, Archie caught a very large fish. The fish was so large that when Archie pulled him out of the water, the water wheel that turned the grindstones quit working. The water level in the mill pond dropped so much that the miller, Luther Morris, yelled at him and made him put the fish back into the water. This raised the water and the grindstones started to work again.

Another story told about Archie was that a young lady that lived about two miles away had mentioned to one of Archie's hunting buddies that she thought she would like to spend some time with Archie. Arrangements were made, a date set in January, and his intentions were to ride Old John over to see this young lady. Getting ready, Archie had his bath and then came into the kitchen to a mirror hanging there on the wall to comb his hair. At that time, his hair was dark brown and somewhat longer than usual. He hadn't had it cut in quite a while. Try as hard as he could with a comb, he just couldn't get his hair to stay in place. He had the idea of putting some warm sausage grease on it. The frying pan was there on the stove with grease in it, still warm from supper. He dipped his fingers into the grease, smoothed it on his hair and combed it. It stayed in place exactly where he wanted it to. Then, he went out into the cold January evening, mounted Old John and rode to the young lady's house. He was met at the door by the young lady's father who looked at Archie in a very odd way and then began to laugh. At this time, his daughter came to the door, saw him and started laughing too. Archie had no idea why they were laughing. He asked why and they escorted him in and gave him a mirror. The sausage grease had turned white. That's what happens to warm sausage grease exposed to cold January weather.

They took him inside to the kitchen, gave him a dish pan of very warm water, soap and towels to get the grease out. Archie continued to see this young lady, Thelma, after he got over his embarrassment.

Hans Krause, his parents and his sister lived in Berlin, Germany. His father was a shoe cobbler and his mother stayed at home. She did a lot of baking and sold these items: pies, strudel, and breads to nearby neighbors. Hans had an uncle, his father's brother, who owned a small farm about forty miles out in the country. Hans spent many days and nights on the farm. The uncle was not well, he had bouts of asthma so bad that he wasn't able to maintain the farm. Hans finally moved there with his uncle and aunt. They had no children of their own so they treated him as if he was theirs. When the seasonal work on the farm was caught up, Hans would travel back to Berlin by train to see his parents and sister. He'd stay there for a few days but was glad to leave and get back to farming. Hans was taught by his uncle how to shoot. He learned quickly and was very good at it. So good was he that he often hunted deer and rabbits successfully. This wild game was welcomed to the daily farm menu.

Throughout Germany, talk of war was the main topic of every conversation. Hitler was by now, 1939, known to all. He was making speeches all over Germany and was encouraging young German men to join the Nazi military. Hans heard the talk in the countryside and some of the speeches when he was visiting his parents in Berlin. There were many of these speeches broadcast on the few radios people had. The more he heard, the more excited he became. He wondered if his skill as a hunter would be appreciated by the army. His parents in Berlin were supportive of Hitler especially when he talked about how bad the Jews were. His older sister had gotten involved with a young Jewish man who had gotten her with child. He then ran out on her, and she lost the baby by miscarriage. This made his parents hate all Jews and by extension, so did Hans. His aunt and uncle on the farm did not feel all Jewish people were bad just because of one. They tried to make this point with Hans, but he would not be convinced.

In 1942, Hans left the farm and joined Hitler's Army, which made his parents proud. Soon, while in training, his skill as a marksman was seen, and he was assigned to a special sniper training group, where he excelled. He fought on the Russian front chalking up many kills and a promotion. He spent time in Poland and the Balkans. By 1944, Sergeant Hans was in France in a foxhole eighty miles inland from Normandy. The D-Day Invasion had occurred three weeks earlier, and the Americans were advancing everywhere. That part of France was mainly farming country with many farmland fields. Between these fields were hedgerows. They were comprised of downed trees, brush and rock piles created when the land was cleared to make the fields. Hedgerows were ideal places to hide troops and weaponry, such as artillery and tanks. Hans and his platoon were dug in beside a large rock pile on one side and a large brush pile on the other side. He was the platoon sniper, and he, with his spotter, was hidden in the brush pile. Hans had been credited with several kills. He was pleased that these Americans would not go home alive.

Some of Archie's schoolmates had already gone off to war. One of his best friends, Maurice Whitlow had left the week before. He knew it was only a matter of time before he was called up. He decided late in 1942 to volunteer to join the Army. He rode to Raleigh for his induction with his father in an old truck Lee had bought the year before. He told Thelma, his girlfriend, Mama, Marilee, and Brindell goodbye.

Archie went through training at Fort Jackson, South Carolina. On the rifle range he scored higher than anyone else day after day. He even won a shooting contest against an Army sergeant who was one of his drill instructors. One day when he was on the range, a Jeep drove up and a captain and his driver got out. The range instructor briefly spoke to the captain, and they both walked over to Archie. He snapped to attention and saluted the captain. He was told to stand at ease, and then the captain asked him if he would like to be part of a special sniper unit. Without hesitation, Archie said yes. The next day he moved his equipment to another part of Fort Jackson called Tank Hill. It was called this because of a large water tank at its top. The captain's name was William "Bill" Sephus. He was in charge of this special unit, and he had several NCO instructors under him.

Archie was given a rifle equipped with a telescopic scope. He had never used one before and had only seen pictures of them. He soon became very proficient with its use. He was trained to work with a spotter. He was told that all good snipers, even the Nazis, worked with a spotter. The spotter was always very close physically to the sniper. The two communicated mainly with hidden hand signals or whispers. The spotter often used binoculars to spot a target. Archie thought back to a hunting trip of several years ago with his Uncle Helon, one of his father's brothers. Uncle Helon was standing beside him in the woods when he first spotted a deer. He loudly shouted, "Deer! Deer! Shoot him! Shoot him!" Archie knew this was certainly different from a real spotter.

While Archie was away in the Army, his brother Brindell and sister Marilee, along with his parents were keeping the farm going. It was especially hard now that Archie was not there to help. There was no local labor to help out, all able-bodied men were serving in the war effort and those too young to serve were helping out their own families.

Marilee, now in her senior year of school, was encouraged by her teacher, Viola Jones, to enter a contest being held county wide. The contest was to select the healthiest high school senior girl. After several weeks of competition to eliminate contestants, she was the only one left. Miss Granville County Health Queen of 1940. She said her good health was certainly not from being pampered, it came from working hard on the farm. By this time, she had a boyfriend, Wilson Dean, who also lived and grew up on a farm.

Marilee did have some competition. There was another young lady who claimed she was in love with Wilson Dean. Wilson drove a school bus in his senior year of school. A young, very pretty lady rode the bus every day, her name was Joyce Daniel. She was a junior. One day there was a pouring rain when the bus got to Joyce's stop, Wilson drove it off the state road. Her house was about a quarter mile from the state road. He knew she would get soaking wet in the walk to her house, so he drove the bus right up to her front porch. There were two quick steps off the bus onto the porch. From that day forward, she said she was in love with Wilson. Wilson's relationship with Marilee was very strong and marriage was often discussed. Wilson got his letter from Uncle Sam to report for his induction into the Army. Two weeks before that date, he and Marilee eloped to Virginia and were married. They spent a short honeymoon in nearby Oxford, North Carolina's only hotel. Needless to say, Marilee's family was not happy with the suddenness of this. Because of the war these sudden marriages did occur more often.

Marilee remained on the farm with her family while Wilson went away for his initial training. He came home on a one-week leave before being shipped out to Europe.

Archie arrived in France two weeks after the initial D-Day Invasion. Prior, he had been at a staging area in England and prior to that in Italy, where he was credited with many kills. His specially trained sniper group was split up with a sniper and his spotter distributed to each infantry platoon. The 2nd Battalion 1st Infantry Division had been pinned down for several days by enemy artillery. They were dug in, in foxholes, but had lost many to enemy fire, especially to a highly skilled enemy sniper. In addition to the losses from the Nazi sniper several had been killed by a stealth assassin. This Nazi's special skills had been responsible for fourteen kills in the unit Archie was assigned to. The killer was able to crawl into the American lines between the hours of 1:00 A.M. and 4:00 A.M. He then killed sleeping soldiers in their foxholes. Ten had been shot and four had their throats cut. Despite everyone being on high alert the assassin was able to slip back out through the lines and get away each time. The next night after the fourteenth kill, Archie was in his foxhole awake while his spotter was taking his turn to sleep. He heard a slight noise nearby and then the sound of a snap, a firing pin hitting a bullet but no shot. The assassin's pistol had misfired. Archie immediately recognized the sound and turned and shot the killer. This kill helped the unit's morale but the sniper was still taking lives. The Company Commander, Captain Wayne Adcock, gave Archie the task of taking out the sniper.

For several days he caught glimpses of the Nazi killer. These glimpses were never long enough for him to set his sights on the target.

Over these few days, the enemy sniper continued to take young American lives. One day, while Archie and his spotter were "glassing" an area in the thickest part of the hedgerow, they saw a movement. The movement was screened by the brush that prevented him from getting a clear shot. After several days, Archie had killed several enemy troops, but not their number one sniper who was still taking American lives. He kept looking at the brushy area where he had seen the screened movement several days earlier. He knew this had to be the sniper's nest.

There was a lull in the battle noise for several hours one day, and he decided to try an old hunting trick. He started whistling at a very low volume. The tune was *Amazing Grace*. He kept this up for twenty minutes with he and his spotter watching everywhere, but especially the brushy area. Slowly, he raised the volume and suddenly he got a clear shot. Immediately he heard yells for help. It was English with an accent of German. The platoon Archie was with waited a couple of hours and then advanced toward the German lines. When they got to the hedgerow, the only person they saw was a wounded sniper. His own spotter had abandoned him. They realized the enemy had already moved out, that's why there was a lull in the battle noise. They had left this sniper to cover their movement and to delay the American advance.

Sergeant Hans Krause had been hit by Archie's bullet in his right side. The bullet had gone through his utility belt, uniform jacket, and lodged near his spine. As he was being seen by American medics, he kept hearing praise for the American who had shot him. They kept congratulating the man, calling him the Double A Whistler, "AA Whistler." Hans didn't know it, but the double A stood for Archie Allen. The congratulations were for the man who had gotten Hitler's best sniper. When Hans was carried back to the aid station by stretcher, he continued to hear the Americans tell others that he was shot by the Double A Whistler.

Unlike American POWs, Nazi POWs were given excellent medical care. Within hours, Hans had surgery, had the bullet removed, and was well on the road to recovery. Forty-five days later, Hans was put on a hospital/POW ship on his way to a POW camp somewhere in the United States. Ironically, he was put on the same ship as some of the Americans he had wounded along with the bodies of dead being returned to their families. Even here on the ship, he was chided as Hitler's best sniper that was brought down by a better sniper, the "Double A Whistler." To rub salt in the wound, some of the Americans started the rumor that the Double A Whistler was Jewish American.

This was not true, but Hans did not know it was not true. When he heard this false rumor, it made him burn with hatred.

Finally, the ship docked in Wilmington, North Carolina, and the POWs were loaded onto trucks for their trip to a camp at Fort Bragg, North Carolina. Within weeks of being in a high-security enclosure at Fort Bragg, the information regarding concentration camps in parts of Europe began to make the news. Photos in newspapers showed emaciated prisoners liberated from camps in Poland. The Americans guarding the POWs at Fort Bragg showed these newspapers to the Nazi POWs. At first Hans didn't believe what he was shown. He thought it was a propaganda trick. As time went on, he started to believe what he saw and heard. He began to wonder how his countrymen could be responsible for something like that. How humans could treat other humans that way. He still believed that the Aryan Nation, Nazis, were superior but given that belief, how could they debase themselves to this level of treatment of others? He knew that even the animals on his uncle's farm were treated better and with more respect. As more news came out over time, his disgust grew.

Over several months, the POWs were questioned one by one regarding their past, their time in the military, and what jobs they had prior to their military service. Their attitude towards their captors was gauged along with their behavior. This was all noted in their record. Ten months after arriving at the Fort Bragg camp, Hans along with 220 other POWs were shipped to a new POW camp at Camp Butner, North

Carolina. This POW camp was near Durham and Creedmoor, North Carolina. Camp Butner was established early in the war to train American troops. The POW camp was built near the US Army training facility. POWs were detailed as maintenance people such as janitorial workers, dishwashers, laundry, etc. Hans was not immediately detailed to work outside the POW compound. He had to go through a "settling in period" where he would closely be observed for his attitude and willingness to cooperate and adhere to rules and instructions.

As time went on, more news came out, this time regarding American POWs that had been liberated. Newspaper pictures showed emaciated American soldiers who were starved and tortured. The Americans guarding Hans and the other POWs were quick to point out the disparity of treatment accorded to them. They received good medical care and were fed well without any intentional mistreatment. In other words, as the guards would say, we treat you as we would want to be treated. This resonated with Hans and most but not all of his fellow POWs.

Wilson, by now, was in Italy with an artillery unit Battery A, 802 BN. The unit was advancing toward the German Border. The fighting was fierce and there were many casualties. He wrote to Marilee and got letters from her. Mostly she talked about what was going on at the farm, about a new calf being born and baby pigs. She wrote about the rationing of gasoline, kerosene, and other items. She said her father was mixing one half kerosene and one half gasoline together because they needed to use the truck to carry tobacco to the market. The gasoline ration by itself did not go far enough to meet their needs. This mix extended the use of the truck but sometimes it was hard to crank. Living on the farm where they raised their own food, there was little other impact. She also wrote regarding Archie and the continued praise he was getting and about his name given to him by his fellow soldiers, "Double A Whistler." She said she had seen Thelma, Archie's girlfriend, at Mt. Zion church many times. They all shared any and all news from him. She said Brindell was seeing someone he seemed to be serious about but was very committed to staying there on the farm to help keep it going until after the war was over. She said their parents Lee and Mary were doing just fine.

Archie's unit was finally out of France and into the countryside of Germany. He had been promoted to sergeant and had received a minor wound from a Nazi grenade fragment. This wound was so minor that the medic, assigned to the unit, put a bandage on it and Archie got back into his sniper's nest. The wound was to his left upper arm and he never mentioned it in his letters home. He told his spotter, Elvin Mangum, that he was once bitten on the leg by one of the hogs at the farm, which was so much worse than the grenade wound. He said he got his revenge when the hog was killed and eaten, great pork chops!

Hans knew that several of his fellow POWs were working out in the community on farms and some were working with local logging crews cutting timber. He talked to three who had been working on the farm of William Jones. They said they were working in tobacco but are now pulling corn, since the tobacco season was over.

They said the work was hard, but they were fed and treated well. Hans, after much thought, asked to speak to the camp commander, Colonel Paul Barrett, to ask permission to work on a farm. He was able to convince Colonel Barrett that he did want to go out working on a farm and that he could be trusted. Since Hans spoke English very well, he thought he would get along fine with an American farmer. The colonel explained that the farmer is given the authority to order the POW to follow instructions. He outlined the rules the POW must adhere to and the consequences he would face if he didn't. Those consequences were being put into solitary confinement and loss of all privileges including a reduction of rations. The colonel explained that the farmers picked up the POWs at the front entrance gate at 8:00 A.M. and had to have them back no later than 7:00 P.M. of the same day. The farmer is given a small pouch containing a photo, description and any other pertinent information about the POW. He further stated that the farmer, Mr. Jones, did not need anyone else but another farmer, Mr. Lee Wilkins, did need two workers and his farm was fourteen miles from the camp. Later that day, Hans talked with one of his fellow POWs, Corporal Werner Tobler, who had been in Han's former unit and had been his spotter when they were on the Russian front. He knew he could trust this fellow soldier and from their many conversations here at the camp, he knew this soldier didn't want to cause trouble. They both just wanted to stay busy to make time pass faster, until the war was over so they could return home.

They knew, as most of the POWs, that the war would soon be over, and Germany was losing. Sergeant Hans went with Corporal Tobler to see the colonel, telling him that he had found another soldier who wanted to work on farmer Lee Wilkins's farm. The colonel gave the corporal the same information he had given Sergeant Hans Krause. Information was sent out to Mr. Wilkins by Jeep messenger. The next morning, there were five POWs waiting to be picked up by farmers. Three were picked up by a Mr. William Daniel for Mr. Jones's farm and Hans and Werner by Mr. Wilkins. Mr. Wilkins got out of his truck at the front entrance wearing faded blue bib overalls. He came over to the men, introduced himself, was told their names and given the information pouch by the second in command, Captain Michael Blair. After these necessary formalities, they drove away.

Hans thought Mr. Wilkins reminded him of his uncle back on the farm in Germany. When they got to the Wilkins home, they were greeted by the rest of the family. Mrs. Wilkins, Mary, seemed to be a very sweet, caring lady. She immediately offered them food, which they declined. The daughter, Marilee was very pretty, but seemed to be a little leery of them as did her brother Brindell. Otherwise, they seemed to be a hard-working farm family. The tobacco season was now over; it had been grown, flue cured, graded, and taken to market and sold. The year was 1945 and it had been a good year for corn. Mr. Wilkins had eight acres of corn and all ears had to be pulled off the stalks by hand. Each stalk had three to four ears of corn. Mr. Wilkins would use this corn to feed cows, pigs, horses, and when ground into cornmeal, to feed the chickens. Some would be carefully cleaned when ground and used in cooking in the house, making delicious corn bread.

Brindell worked along with Hans, Werner, and Mr. Wilkins. There was no language problem for Hans, he had been taught English in school in Germany. Werner was not as proficient as Hans, so Hans translated for him as needed. At midmorning, Mr. Wilkins's daughter, Marilee came out to the field carrying water in a large jug along with some apples. Mr. Wilkins, Lee, said they were grown on the farm. Brindell often spoke but only to his father. He continued to keep his distance from the POWs. A little after 12:00 noon, they heard a bell ring twice. Lee said it was the call to come to the house to eat. In this part of the south, the noon meal was called "dunna"—this stood for dinner. They tied Old John, who was hitched to the wagon loaded with corn to a tree near the end of the corn row. They walked the short distance to the house. Hans and Werner were shown into an enclosed back porch where they would wash the field dirt off their hands with the wash pan and towels there.

Mrs. Wilkins, Mary, invited them into the kitchen where a large round table was set with plates and silverware for all. Hans had not expected to be able to eat at the same table with the family. He was surprised and pleased at the same time. It made him feel more human and less like a captured prisoner. He and Werner sat side by side with Mr. Wilkins on one side of them. On the other side of Mr, Wilkins sat his daughter, Marilee, then Mrs. Wilkins, then Brindell. Between Brindell and Werner was an empty chair. The seating arrangement shouted clearly that Mr. Wilkins and his son would protect the women who sat between them. Mr. Wilkins offered a prayer of thanks for the food.

The food, fried chicken, green beans, fried potatoes, and corn bread was delicious and plentiful. The dessert, was a small piece of chocolate pie for each. After eating, the four men walked back to the field and went back to pulling corn. At 5:00 P.M. they left the field riding on the wagon loaded with corn, pulled by Old John. They unloaded the corn into the corncrib and were then driven back to the POW camp.

Hans and Werner felt good about the day, the food, and the interaction with the family. They commented to each other about the pretty daughter, Marilee and the fact that she was married to an American soldier. This they had learned from talk around the dunna table. They also learned that there was a son of the family who was a soldier. The next several days were a repeat of the first, the only variation was the menu and the midmorning snack. Brindell had loosened up some when he heard Hans talking about living and working on his uncle's farm. He even asked what crops and animals were on the farm. Conversations at the dunna table were more relaxed with each passing day. The meal was always preceded by a prayer of thanks from Lee.

On Friday, they stopped working at 3:00 P.M., rode the wagon to the corncrib building, unloaded it, and put Old John in his stable. Mr. Wilkins then gave them a quick tour of the barn lot where the cows, horses, and pigs were kept. They saw the pasture where the cows and horses were turned into from the barn and stable. They saw the chicken pen, tobacco barns, and pack house where all the tobacco was put after it was cured, then graded, and taken to market. They saw the hayloft adjacent to the stables.

Monday was a repeat of the week before. It was going to be that way until all the corn was pulled and put into the crib. The dunna meal was always delicious and sometimes the mid-morning snack in the field was cold water and a fried apple pie or a pear. When Marilee brought them out, she often stayed awhile to talk to all, often smiling at Hans. Mr. Wilkins quickly reminded her that she had work to do back at the house and sent her on her way.

Hans began to notice that Old John was indeed getting old and seemed to be losing weight each week. He also had a harder time pulling the weight of the fully loaded wagon. Hans talked to Mr. Wilkins and Brindell about it and told them that his uncle once had a horse that showed the same condition and it had to be put down. Brindell spoke up and said he hoped it would not come to that.

Three weeks later, the routine remained the same except Old John just couldn't pull the loaded wagon anymore. Mr. Wilkins had another horse that was several years younger but not as mindful as Old John. He started using this horse. He was named Cal, after one of Mr. Wilkins's seven brothers. He needed some yelling and snapping the reins across his back, burning his hide some before he got into the routine. Each day, Marilee would go out to the stable to see Old John, taking him apples and talking to and petting him. Each day he seemed to get a little worse.

By now, of course, Hans and Werner knew more about the other son whose name was Archie. They were shown a picture of him made a couple of years before he went off to war. Hans thought somehow he looked vaguely familiar. They also saw a picture of Marilee's husband, Wilson. They knew that both of the men were fighting against their countrymen. Letters from Archie and Wilson both said they were now entering Germany. When discussing these letters, the reader, usually Marilee, left out information and words such as, "Krauts" killed or captured. She knew those words would only make things uncomfortable for Hans and Werner and would create tension between all of them.

Most of the talk about Archie was about his hunting skills. They did, however, mention the incident about the sausage grease. This got a laugh all around. As was often the case, Hans had to do some translation for Werner and once done his laughter joined in.

The next week on Thursday, Marilee came running out to the cornfield upset. She said Old John was down in the stable and could not get up. They all loaded into the wagon and went to the stable. Mr. Wilkins told Brindell to go with Hans and Werner to the house and go sit on the front porch. After they had left, he told Marilee to go into the house to get his rifle and come out the back door with it so those on the front porch would not see it. She brought the rifle to the stable and said her goodbyes to Old John, re-membering all the times he was ridden to school, all the times he walked with his head inside the rear of the school bus, and the cowboy and Indian chases. She left the stable crying as she heard the shot. She ran towards the front of the house, with tears streaming from her eyes, and she stumbled and fell. Hans ran off the porch and picked her up and held her in his arms as she sobbed. Brindell quickly came over and pulled her into his arms.

They did not go back to the cornfield that day, but Hans and Werner helped hook up Cal to Old John and drag him off to a far corner of the farm, far enough away that they would not be able to see the buzzards or smell the stench of death. That's how dead farm animals were done in that time.

The next week, the POWS were restricted to the camp. There had been an escape over the weekend and authorities there at the camp and law enforcement outside wanted to do an investigation. They needed to be sure it wasn't part of a larger escape plot and they wanted to see if others were involved, still inside. After that week, all was back to normal except when Mr. Wilkins went to pick up Hans and Werner. Only Hans was at the front gate. Mr. Wilkins was told by the gate guard, Staff Sergeant Douglas Denny, that POW Werner Tobler was sick and would not be working again until he was well. This put an extra workload on Lee, Brindell, and Hans.

By now, the dunna meal was even more enjoyable. All were relaxed and seemed to enjoy the company of Hans, especially when he talked about his uncle's farm. Even Brindell was friendly. Jokes and funny stories were told with laughter by all. Several times during these moments, Marilee touched Hans's foot under the table with hers. Mrs. Wilkins had on several occasions made vegetable soup with homegrown vegetables. Hans said it was the best he'd ever eaten and asked for the recipe to be written down so he could take it him back to Germany. This brought an awkward silence, which was quickly broken by Mr. Wilkins saying it would be even better if it had some possum meat in it.

Another thing Hans and Werner watched with interest at every meal was Lee make his special soppings, as he called it. After he had finished his meal and his plate was fairly clean, he would pour sweet corn syrup on it. He then added some butter and stirred it vigorously with a fork until it was a golden color. Next he would take a half of a biscuit and drag part of it through the mixture; if it broke apart he said it was too thick. He then added more syrup, stirred it again and repeated the process until the bread did not break apart. It was then declared "just right" and eaten as his dessert. He often used the word "suffice" whenever something met his approval or satisfaction. When he made this sweet dessert, he sometimes would say "that will suffice" just before he ate it. This too brought on laughter and a foot touch under the table. Hans knew this was no accident. Hans knew by now he had an attraction to Marilee and he felt sure it was mutual. He knew he had to behave himself because he was a POW and she was married; married to a soldier and was the sister of a soldier fighting in his country against his people.

The next week, Werner was well enough to work again, so again they pulled corn. It was going well and they only had about one and a half acres left, which would take about three more weeks, weather permitting. That weekend in camp, Hans told Werner of his feelings towards Marilee and that he thought she had the same towards him. Werner cautioned him because even he could sense something from their relationship. Werner suggested Hans get off this farm detail and get on another one. Hans said he would give that some thought.

On Monday, Hans and Werner were waiting to be picked up. This time, Brindell picked them up stating that his father was a bit under the weather. He told them on the way out to the farm that when they came home from church the day before, Lee said he just didn't feel good. He did not eat the dunna meal, supper, or breakfast this morning. When they got to the farm, Brindell went to check on his father. Lee said he felt better but was not up to pulling corn. Before going out to the field, Hans stated he needed to go to the "outhouse" (outside toilet). On his way there, he met Marilee who was just returning from the outhouse. They stopped and chatted just a moment about Lee. She told him she appreciated his concern and quickly kissed his cheek while touching his hand. As they stood there, they heard someone walking down the path towards them. They quickly moved apart and went their separate ways. It was Brindell but he only saw them a good distance apart from each other. When Hans told Werner about this, he was quick again to warn him to be careful.

The three of them worked to dunna, ate fried pork chops, mashed potatoes with gravy, green beans, and biscuits. Afterwards, Brindell said he needed their help to hook up Cal to the plow so the potatoes could be plowed out of the ground. He told Marilee they would need her help in picking up the potatoes.

By 5:00 P.M., three rows of potatoes were finished with a gathering of three bushels. It seems that Hans and Marilee bumped into or brushed up against each other several times when bending over to pick up potatoes. Werner later said it was too may times to have been accidental. Cal was put in the stable, the potatoes in the pack barn, and Hans and Werner were taken back to the POW camp.

That evening, Marilee sat beside her father on the front porch while Mary was in the kitchen cleaning up from supper and baking pies. Brindell was away, gone to visit a young lady he often sat with at church. Her name was Maria Rose, sister of Doug Vaughn, a good friend of Brindell's. Lee said they were lucky to get Hans and Werner to help out on the farm while Archie was off at war. He said that the POWs were hard workers and almost fit in like added family members. He also said they would probably be going back to Germany within a year's time, with the war coming to an end. He reminded Marilee that Wilson would be returning home too, after the war and they could start a family. He said, "I can see you have some affection for Hans, but you are a married woman. Married to Wilson."

Marilee realized from her father's comments that her feelings for Hans must now be somewhat visible to all. She knew she needed to be very careful.

The next day, Lee still wasn't up to working, so Marilee, Brindell, Hans, and Werner finished harvesting the potatoes, gathering three more bushels. It was a couple of hours earlier than when they usually quit for the day, but it was still too late to start on something else. Brindell said he would put Cal in the stable, they would wash up and go sit on the front porch until it was time to take Hans and Werner back to camp. Before he could get Cal in the stable, a neighbor, Harry Newton, drove up in his truck saying he needed Mr. Wilkins help right away. He said one of his cows was stuck in the mud in his pond and she was trying to birth a calf. Brindell told him that his father was sick, but he would go help him. He turned to Hans and Werner and told them to put Cal in the stable, put water in one trough and hay in the other. He jumped into his neighbor's truck, as they drove away, he yelled to Marilee that if he didn't get back by six o'clock, she would have to take Hans and Werner back to camp, and if Daddy didn't feel well enough to go, Mama should ride along.

Hans led Cal to the stable, Marilee followed, and Werner stopped outside the stable and sat down on a tree stump where he could clearly see the house and the driveway. Marilee followed Hans inside to the hayloft. They got down the hay for Cal, stopped, and held each other, and gently kissed. They kissed again with more urgency, this kiss turned to passion and then it happened. They made love in the hayloft. Almost as soon as it started it was over, but not because of the cold weather. Marilee ran upset from the stable and hayloft toward the house with tears in her eyes. Mary saw her and asked what had happened. She said she had fallen and that it had hurt, but she knew nothing was broken. She then went to the outhouse where she could cry, calm down, and compose herself. Within the hour, Brindell was back saying they had gotten the cow out of the pond, and she immediately gave birth to a healthy calf. He took Hans and Werner back to the POW camp, telling them that he or Lee would pick them up Monday morning.

That weekend was strangely quiet. Lee was back to his healthy self again. Church on Sunday was as usual with Mary singing in the choir. This Sunday, they sang her favorite hymn, *Amazing Grace*. Marilee was contrite and as the hymn was sung, she began to quietly cry while keeping it hidden from everyone.

Monday morning, Lee picked up only Werner. The sergeant at the front entrance, Sergeant Ezra Hardesty, informed Lee that Hans was ill and had gone on sick call that morning. Lee thought maybe Hans had caught what he had just gotten over. When Lee arrived at the farm with only Werner, Marilee was relieved. She felt so conflicted with what she had done, her feelings for Hans and her husband Wilson and the guilt.

On Thursday morning, Lee picked up both Hans and Werner. This was the first day Hans was back to work. When he saw Marilee, he wanted to run to her, take her into his arms, but he knew better. Later, in the day, just before dunna, while no one else was in hearing range, they both apologized to each other and agreed to keep their distance.

The next day, Friday, was as usual, hard farmwork. At dunna, Marilee opened a letter from brother Archie. There were only two pages. In block letters on the first page it said, THE WAR IS OVER! On the second page, in block letters, it said, THE DOUBLE A WHISTLER IS COMING HOME.

Hans could hardly believe it, now he knew why that picture of Archie looked familiar. Archie was the sniper that shot him. He had worked for the family of the man that shot him. All this time, he had worked for the father of the, "Double A Whistler." He had worked alongside his brother and had fallen in love with his sister. This man who shot him is the one he was taunted about and yet he had eaten at his mother's table.

When the celebrating was over, Hans asked about Archie and what the double A stood for. Archie Allen, he was told. Then he was told about the whistler part and the hymn, *Amazing Grace*. Marilee said the men in his platoon put it all together and coined the name, Double A Whistler. Hans could hardly believe what fate had thrown at his feet and his heart. What were the odds of getting shot in France so far away, then ending up on the farm of the fellow who had shot him? All because of a hymn being whistled and of course now knowing Archie was not Jewish as he had been told.

When they got back to camp, the place was in an uproar over the news about the war being over, it had been broadcast over the camp's public address system. All the guards were talking about it. Hans was still in shock about what he had just learned at the Wilkins's kitchen table. He could only sit on his bunk thinking about it and shaking his head in disbelief. He now had the whole weekend to take this in.

There were several announcements over the weekend from the authorities of the camp. They held a meeting with all the POWs under the large enclosed tent. They advised all that they would have to wait for orders from Washington regarding the repatriation of the POWs. Until then, everything would continue as before. Over the weekend, a delegation of Swiss and Red Cross inspectors toured the camp headed by Mr. Wallace Bowling and Ms. Ava Hardesty. They were pleased with the activities afforded to the POWs, the sanitation, and rations provided. They said this would be the last inspection.

Hans penned a letter to his aunt and uncle and one to his parents. He did not mention his dilemma regarding Marilee. He advised he would write again when he could talk about when he was coming home. All weekend he stewed over the situation, Werner was no help, had no sympathy, just kept saying, "I told you to be careful."

The next week was hard. The farmwork was easy compared to the existing feelings and those to come. The POWs were told that this would be their last week working outside the camp. In every instance, they had been treated well, with respect and had worked hard. They were fed well and cared for medically. Many had become very close to the families they had worked for, almost as extended family members. This was the case with Hans, Werner, and the Wilkins family.

On Thursday, their last day on the farm, they all sat talking around the kitchen table. Brindell had a camera he had borrowed from Clyde Hicks. He took pictures of everyone together and then one of just Hans and Werner. Hans again told everyone about the farm his aunt and uncle owned and that they were giving it to him. He told them it was about forty miles south of Berlin in a small village named Pertz. He even invited them all to someday visit after any needed reconstruction was completed. Hans and Werner hugged Mrs. Wilkins and thanked her for the wonderful meals she had fed them. Brindell and Marilee walked outside with them towards the truck. They shook Brindell's hand, said their goodbyes, and he went back inside the house.

Hans reached in his pocket and took out a small copper coin. He showed it to Marilee and said it was a coin given to him by his grandfather many years ago. He said it was supposed to be a good luck coin and it had been his great-great-grandfather's. He said you could still see the date of 1785 on it but most of the other letters were worn off. Hans said he had been searched when he was shot and captured and it was found. When he told his captors it was his good luck coin, they laughed and said it must not be working. His thoughts were that maybe it kept him from being killed. Each time he was moved, to the ship, to Fort Bragg, and to Butner, his captors searched him. He was searched every time he returned from work detail. Each time the coin was found, he never tried to hide it and always kept it with him. When found, he told them it was his good luck coin and each time they laughed at him and let him keep it. The guards there at Camp Butner were now used to finding it and said little about it. He then gave the coin to Marilee and told her the coin in its convoluted way brought him to her. He asked her to keep it to remember him by. Marilee turned to walk away with tears in her eyes. She took ten steps, then turned around, ran back to Hans and embraced him. They stood like this holding each other until they heard the kitchen door slam. She broke away and ran to the stable. In the hayloft, she sat there listening to the truck as it was started and was driven away by her father with Hans and Werner. She knew that she would probably never see Hans Krause again, as she held the coin tightly, wet with her tears.

A week later, Archie came home. His girl-friend, Thelma along with many family and friends, came to welcome him home. They had a big celebration with lots of food and a prayer of thankfulness. They could hardly believe he had been wounded and had not written about it in his letters. At the end of the day, he and Thelma announced that they were officially engaged to be married and a date was set for six weeks later.

Later that evening, after he had taken Thelma home and all of the visitors had left, he and Marilee talked. She talked about the two POWs that had worked there for several months. She told him their names. When she said Sergeant Hans Krause, she detected immediate attention by Archie. She told him he should recognize the name. "He told us on the day we opened your two-page letter and read it at the kitchen table—the letter saying, THE WAR IS OVER – THE DOUBLE A WHISTLER IS COMING HOME, Hans said that was the name of the soldier that shot him."

Archie, as Hans had before, could hardly believe the situation that had brought all this together here at his family's farm in Berea, North Carolina. The odds of this happening were almost unbelievable.

Three weeks later, Wilson came home. When Marilee saw him, she forgot about Hans and her heartache. As at the Wilkins's home weeks before, a celebration was held at Mr. and Mrs. Billy Dean's farmhouse, this was the other of the two Dean homeplaces. This one was at the junction of the Bob Daniel and Dean Road. Wilson's three sisters, Julia, Ruth, and Inez, with her husband Garland were there along with many neighbors and friends. Wilson and Marilee moved in with his parents while a small wooden frame house was being built for them by farmhands and neighbors. The house was built across the state road directly in front of the home place. Within a few weeks, Marilee realized she was going to have a baby. When the new house was finished early in 1946, it had no indoor plumbing or electricity. The outhouse was just a few steps away out back with the well on the other side of the house. It had a bucket with a chain attached to pull up the water.

Wilson worked on the farm with his father, Billy and Inez's husband. Billy was a deacon in the church and a Sunday School teacher. Each Sunday morning, before it was time to leave for church, he would go out into the barn lot where he rehearsed his Sunday School lesson. There, surrounded by five large log tobacco barns he loudly preached the gospel. Mary, Wilson's mother, was widely known for baking the best gingerbread men in the area. She took care of their vegetable garden in summer and always fed the chickens and gathered their eggs.

Ruth and Julia lived together in Maryland, just outside Washington, DC. Ruth worked and Julia maintained the home.

After a few months, Wilson was able to buy a used car, which he sometimes drove when he had too much to drink. This occurred on weekends when he wasn't busy on the farm. This behavior of sometimes drinking too much started when he was in the Army.

Marilee began to have labor pains on November 16, but luckily Inez was there visiting. Wilson was away somewhere. Inez went across the road and told Mr. and Mrs. Dean. She got Garland and they took Marilee to the hospital in Oxford. Oxford was the county seat and the closest large city to the Dean home near Berea. There, she was placed in the maternity ward. Several hours later, Wilson was put in the same hospital on the next floor down. He had gotten home and read the note about Marilee being taken to the hospital in labor. Unfortunately, he had been drinking earlier and wrecked the car on the way to the hospital.

Marilee gave birth to a healthy boy just after midnight. Jerry Wayne Dean was born on November 17, 1946. Within a few days, all three went home.

GROWING UP

The following is history as told to me many years later.

After the next year's tobacco crop was finished and sold, we moved to Maryland. Daddy had taken a job as farm manager at the Stone Ridge School of the Sacred Heart. It was a thirty-five-acre convent/farm. My mother taught the nuns and other staff how to "put up" can vegetables from their gardens. She also chauffeured the nuns any place they needed to go including all over Washington, DC. Often when Mama was doing things for the sisters away from the convent other sisters would babysit me.

After this job, Daddy took another in Maryland, again as the farm manager for a Mr. Raply. This was a large farm of mostly dairy cattle and some supportive crops. We moved into a nice brick home that was just for the farm manager. It had indoor plumbing and electricity. Of course, I do not remember this move but this is where my first conscious memory takes place. I remember bending over, above a chamber pot, looking between my legs and watching worms come out of me and fall into the pot. At this age, two or close to three, this was fascinating. Mama had given me medicine the day before, to "worm me."

The second memory was also at this same place. I was eating applesauce, while in a high chair. I started rocking the chair back and forth, it turned over and spilled applesauce all over me. I still to this day, seventy-three-some years later, do not care for applesauce.

GRANDMA'S PLACE

Living at Grandma's (Grandma Wilkins) was my next memory. I don't remember the move from Maryland back to North Carolina. Grandma's place was just outside of Stem North Carolina, on what is now Tump Wilkins Road. Tump was Grandma's husband, and they were my great grandparents. Tump and Grandma raised eight boys in the old two-story farmhouse that had no indoor plumbing or electricity. One of these boys was my grandfather Willie Lee Wilkins, my mama's father. When we lived there, the house still had no indoor plumbing or electricity. It was heated in the winter with fires in heaters, fireplace, and wood cookstove.

We farmed tobacco and raised hogs and chickens to eat. We did have a few turkeys and at one time, several white rabbits. I remember digging in the dirt, at the base of a pecan tree, which was beside the path (driveway) to the house, from the state road. There were several pecan trees in a row. Daddy was plowing land beside the row of pecan trees. I was playing under one, when I dug up a Pepsi Cola bottle that had never been opened. I don't know why or how it came to be buried, but to me it was like finding gold. We were poor, and I seldom got something like a cola of any type. I finally got it opened and drank it all.

I remember Daddy killing a wild turkey, in the barn lot. It was mating season and one of our tame turkeys started calling to the wild one. The tame one convinced the wild one to come for a romantic rendezvous. Instead, he was meat on our table.

One day, Mama wanted Daddy to catch one of our barn lot chickens, so she could kill and fix it for the supper table. He chased and chased, couldn't catch it, so he went inside, got the shot gun and shot the chicken. We had chicken that night for supper. For a while, we had several white rabbits in a pen outside. They dug out and escaped but started living under a building we called a pack house. This building is where we graded tobacco and readied it for the market. Over time Daddy caught or killed all of them, for the cook pot. We all loved eating rabbit, and when the white ones were all gone, Daddy came up with an idea to get more rabbit meat. Our house was at the end of a long driveway from the state road. It was about 1/4 mile long. At night, when we were going in or out of the driveway, we always saw wild rabbits run across it. Daddy got Mama to drive the car, while he sat on the front edge of the car's hood, resting his feet on the bumper. In his hand was the shotgun. As rabbits ran across the driveway, he would shoot them. There were times when he killed as many as five in one night. Mama did all the cooking, on a wood-fired cook-stove that sat diagonally across a corner, in the kitchen. This provided a large triangular space behind it, to the corner of the room. I would often crawl back behind the stove, especially in the winter. I hid and stayed warm too. Looking under the stove, I could see anyone's feet who came into the kitchen, without them seeing me. I also loved to hide under the table that sat on the back porch. We called it a water table because it always had a bucket of water with a dipper in it. Everyone drank from this bucket, using the same dipper. There was also a wash pan beside the bucket, used by every-one to wash their hands.

At the end of the driveway, where it con-nected to the state road, was the home of Uncle Cal and his family. Uncle Cal was one of my granddaddy's brothers. He had a wife, two daughters, and two sons. The youngest son Raymond was about the same age as me. I would often make the walk up to Raymond's house where we would play cowboys and In-dians. We also would make wine, or at least what we called wine. We took pokeberries, crushed them in a can to get their red juices, and then we would add water to it in the jar. It looked just like wine. Somehow, we knew it was poison and it would kill us if we drank it, so we didn't.

For a year or so, we had an older white man living with us, in an upstairs room. His name was Mr. Bumpas. He lived with us to help with the growing, curing, and grading of tobacco. He was a big likable man, who laughed easily and loved to eat cabbage. He seemed old to me, but I was only four or five. In his spare time, he made walking sticks. When not working, he and I would spend countless hours walking in the woods. He was looking for small trees that had vines growing around them, which gave the tree a spiral twist. He would cut these down, pull the vines off, peel the bark off and do some whittling on it and let it dry out. He made beautiful canes, but I never knew what he did with all of them. While we tramped through the woods looking for the right twisted tree for him to make a cane, we also looked for terrapins, and we found many. I always took them home, kept them for a few days, and then turned them loose.

We had a corn shucking there at Grandma's place one fall. The yard was filled with piles of corn, straight from the field, still in the shuck. All of our nearby neighbors and relatives came over to help shuck corn. Some of the women helped but several were in the house fixing different things to go in a large cast iron pot, to make Brunswick stew that was cooked there in the yard. At the end of the day, all the corn was shucked, put in the corncrib and all of us were full of stew.

I took baths in the kitchen. Mama would heat water on the wood cookstove and then pour it into a large galvanized tin tub on the floor. I bathed in these tubs a couple of times a week or more if needed like when I played in mud puddles.

The MANGUM FARM

My next memory is of moving to another farm, owned by Mr. Otha Mangum. We moved there as sharecroppers growing tobacco. The house we moved into was a white, wooden, two-story house. This house also had no electricity or running water inside. Right after we moved in, a new outhouse had to be built with the necessary large hole dug beneath it. It was built beside the chicken lot so when you were sitting there meditating, looking at the toilet paper (Sears and Roebuck Catalog), you could be serenaded by the clucking chickens. I was between five and six years old. Mama cooked on the same old cast iron wood-fired cookstove we had used at Grandma's place. It had moved with us. The house had no insulation and was heated by wood-burning heaters. We still bathed in the galvanized tin tubs after the water was heated. This house was very cold in the wintertime. The house sat a half a mile from the state road. This state road is now named Jack Clement Road. I had to walk half a mile from our house to the state road to catch the school bus.

This of course was a twice-a-day ordeal. I started school in 1952, so I had to make the trip daily. Where our road met the state road, there was a large white two-story wooden house. The family that lived there were the Ellises. I later learned that my mother's mother, my grandmother, grew up in that same house. She was Mary Bowling then. The Ellises let me wait on the porch for the school bus. This was great, especially when it was raining. One day in 1952, school was closed early because of a hurricane coming our way. This was Hurricane Hazel. I got off the bus in hurricane winds and ran to the Ellis porch and Mrs. Ellis told me to come inside. I stood just inside the house while watching huge oak trees blow down in the front and side yards. It was scary.

A year earlier, a colored, (this was the term used at this time period) family moved into another tenant house on the farm. It was a small house, having five rooms, which included the kitchen. The family consisted of one adult, the mother named Liss, and her six boys and four girls. The two oldest boys were in their early twenties and were to help Daddy on the farm. These two young men were Wallace and Junior. They ate their noon meal at our house, in the kitchen, after my family had eaten. This was the custom at the time, while they were working on the farm. The other boys were Erba Lee, who had the biggest feet of anyone his age I had ever seen. He was always tripping over his own feet. Next was Elleck, then Nelson, then my best buddy Booty Boy. The name Booty Boy did not have the same connotation as it does now. Booty boy was a friend if I ever had one. He looked out for me. I'm guessing he was about eight and I was six. The girls were Suzy Mae, Gertrude,

Florine, and Lilly Bee. Suzy Mae and Gertrude often helped Mama in the garden and with canning vegetables. We all shared what the garden produced. Liss didn't do much cooking. When one of the children said they were hungry, she told them to go fix themselves something.

At six years old, I was outside roaming in the woods, along the creeks most of the time, unless there were chores to be done, like bringing in the wood for cooking or heating, or going to the spring to bring in water to the house. If not doing chores or going to school, winter or summer, I was in the woods with Booty Boy. Most of the time, Elleck and Nelson were along too. Erba Lee went sometimes, but his favorite thing was to sleep. In the summer of 1952, we spent hours damming up the stream that was the outflow of the spring where we all got our drinking water. We dammed it up to create a swimming hole.

We played in it all the hot summer. This spring was at the bottom of a hill and we all had to carry buckets of water up the hill to our houses, several times a day if Mama was washing clothes or if we had to take a bath. Since I was a little tyke, I carried two three-pound buckets (buckets that lard had been in). The total distance to the house was about thirty yards uphill and seventy yards on flat ground. Liss's house was at the top of the hill, so her crew didn't carry water as far as I did.

In late 1952, a well was dug near the house and electricity was put in the well house for the pump, and in the house for the lighting. In the early part of 1953, a bathroom was put in the house and a kitchen sink with running water in it. I was so happy that I didn't have to use the outhouse anymore, especially in the cold winter. With the new bathroom, I was able to bathe in a real bathtub and not a galvanized tin tub. With electricity in the house, Mama got an electric stove, a refrigerator and an upright freezer to keep the vegetables and meat in.

In addition to swimming, we spent the summers trying to find and catch a baby crow. Booty Boy had been told, by someone he trusted, that if you caught a baby crow and split its tongue, you could teach it to talk. Of course, if Booty Boy believed it, I did also. We walked through all the nearby woods, all summer, with our heads tilted back, looking for a crow's nest. We found many nests, some Booty boy climbed up to, only to find it occupied by a squirrel. One trip, Erba Lee went with us and Booty Boy was able to convince him to climb up to the nest. Before he started to climb, he said if there was a baby crow, it was his. He got up to the nest and reached up to see what was in it. At that instant, a large black snake came out of the nest and fell right on Erba Lee's head. I have never heard such an anguished yell that ended when he fell to the ground. Luckily the nest was only about fifteen feet up. We never had a chance to see if he was hurt, he was up and running towards the house as fast as those big feet would carry him. We never did catch a baby crow that summer or the next.

Mr. Mangum, that owned the farm, was a very likable man. He owned a brick general store in Stem, North Carolina, and Daddy and I often stopped by to see him. He was always very nice to me. He would often give me candy when we were in the store. Years later, Mama told me that Mr. Mangum had lost his only son in WWII, and he asked Mama if she would sell me to him. She said he told her he wanted a son again and he would pay well for me. She refused. I'm sure many years later, after some of my antics as a teenager, she wished she had taken him up on his offer.

During this time, my family did not know where I was when I was out of the house, or if I was safe. They knew two things, if I was with Booty Boy, he would look out for me and that l would always come home when I got hungry. I would have and could have eaten at Booty Boy's house but as told earlier, his mother didn't fix much food. Suzy Mae did most of the food preparation and Erba Lee and Gertrude ate most of it.

The only time I got hurt while out with Booty Boy, was once when we were again trying to find a baby crow. We were walking along an old farm road and we saw what looked like a small trash dump beside it. There were some #10 cans in the dump; the large ones the size that vegetables and other stuff comes in when delivered to schools and hospitals. We started throwing the cans up in the air and trying to hit them with rocks while they were up. One of the cans came down and hit me in the forehead, just at the edge of my hair. The part of the can that hit me was where the lid had been torn off and it was sharp. The jagged edge cut a large gash in my head and it bled like a running river. Booty Boy, Elleck, Nelson and I thought I was going to die. Elleck made me promise that I wouldn't come back from the dead and "haint" (haunt) him. Nelson found a snot rag in his pocket, soaked it in a small stream and put it on my head. I thanked him for saving my life. We went back home through the woods; they went straight to their house; afraid they might get blamed for my accident. They didn't. Mama put a Band-Aid on it.

In our wanderings, we learned that you could go through the woods on the back side of the farm, and if you walked long enough, you came out on another state road (now called Enon Church Road). On the road was a country store owned by Tetum Evans. He sold among many things, fresh eggs.

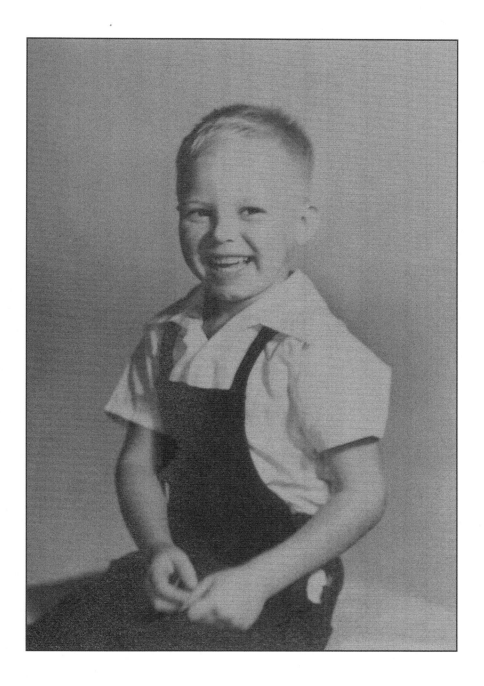

THE GOLD RING (PLASTIC)

One day Booty Boy showed me his beautiful gold ring he had on his finger, and I asked him where he got it. He said he traded Mr. Evans several fresh eggs for round sticks of bubble gum. The sticks were the size and length of a finger, and every fifth one had a gold finger ring on it. I told him I wanted a ring like that. He said he would get some eggs to trade. I asked him where he got his eggs, and he said he got them from the Ellis's. For several months after that I was part of the egg heist gang, with Booty Boy and crew. The crew was Booty Boy, Elleck, Nelson, Erba Lee, and I.

On weekends or summer vacation from school, we would wander down towards the Ellis house. If their car was gone, we knew they too were gone. When we saw they were away, we went to the chicken pen. This was a hen house about 10 X 15 with a yard area and an 8 tall fence around it. The hen house had tin wash tubs hanging on the back outside and nesting boxes for laying, inside. We would first get the eggs out of all the nests and put them in a sack. If a chicken was on the nest, we would pick her up, start squeezing her at the front chest, working the squeeze toward her rear. This actually pushed the egg out if it was close to coming out anyway. The chickens repeatedly voiced their dislike for this procedure. If we couldn't squeeze it out, we would take down a tub from the back wall and put the chicken under the upside tub and wait for it to lay. Now looking back, I'm seventy-three years old now, that had to be some sight. Three colored boys and one white boy, sitting around a wash tub in a circle, waiting for a chicken to lay an egg so we could steal it and trade if for bubble gum that had a gold ring around it.

Whenever we did this, we got Erba Lee to go with us. He was the lookout man. He went out next to the state road and sat beside a tree so he could see if their car was coming down the road. He always let us know if they were coming home, so we could hang up the tub if we were using one and get out of the pen and out of the area or at least out of sight. We almost got caught once. We were sitting around the tub, with a chicken under it, when we heard their car door slam. We got up and ran, leaving the tub and the chicken on the ground. Luck was that they always parked the car on one side of that large house, and the chicken pen was on the opposite side. When the car door slammed, it woke up Erba Lee, our lookout. It seemed he was doing one of his favorite things, sleeping. I thought a lot about this over the years, wondering if the Ellises thought their chickens had periods when they didn't lay eggs (because we had gotten all of them out of the nests). They had to be perplexed to see a tin wash tub on the ground inside the pen, and especially to find a chicken under it. Maybe it could be rationalized with the wind blowing the tub off its nail hanger and just as it was falling to the ground, a chicken walked under it and it scared the chicken so bad it laid an egg. I also wondered how many different kinds of chicken feed they bought in order to boost their egg laying.

Suzy Mae was an entrepreneur; a salesman came by every so often and sold her stale candy at a cheap rate. She would keep the candy locked up in an old wooden footlocker. She would sell candy to her brothers, her sisters and anyone else who happened by. I bought a piece every once in a while, on the rare occasions when I had a nickel. One piece was a flat bar of coconut that had colors of the rainbow on it. I seldom had candy in those days and even though it was stale, it was good. Erba Lee never had money to buy Suzy Mae's candy and he always begged her for candy. One day when she was picking beans in the garden, he busted open the lock on the footlocker and sat there beside it and ate about sixteen candy bars, leaving the wrappers on the floor. That was the last of Suzy Mae's candy business. I think she would have killed her brother if it hadn't been for Liss stopping her.

During the hottest part of the summer, we took a break from crow hunting and chasing butterflies. Instead we spent time in the swimming hole. We would often get inside an old tire and roll down the hill to the spring and the swimming hole. Many times, the tire rolled right into the spring or the swimming hole. This was a lot of fun. When you first came down the hill, walking toward the spring, you would often see a flurry of brown fur. I later learned that these were mink after I saw a picture of one in a book.

Booty Boy and his brothers taught me that the things in the water, with claws and shells on its body were craw devils. They were afraid of them and taught me to fear them too. I learned years later that they were crayfish. Many times, when we got in the swimming hole, we would get small leeches on us. We would let them fill up with our blood then slap them so they would burst. Occasionally, we found a snake in the hole. We ran away and didn't stop until we got to the top of the hill.

THE TASTE OF BUTTERFLY HEADS

The taste of butterfly heads is terrible. I know this because every summer I bit the heads off dozens of butterflies. Booty Boy and his brothers believed in an old superstition that if you caught a butterfly, bit off its head and threw the butterfly over your shoulder and didn't look back, you would get a new suit of clothes. In those days, as tenant farmers and sharecroppers, we didn't have much more than hand-me-downs or work clothes to wear. So, the mysterious promise of a new suit of clothes was worth the lives of many, many butterflies. Unfortunately, it didn't work.

SCHOOL

I did like school when I started in the first grade at Stem. Not the study and learning part but all the new foods at lunch and all the girls. That first year, I fell in love with a blonde classmate named Diane Jost. I proposed to her and she accepted after only knowing her for a couple of months. Before the end of the school year, she moved away, and I was heartbroken. Soon I fell in love with another classmate, Linda Bowling. This lasted several months until I told Mama about Linda, and she said, "You can't marry her because she is a distant cousin." Her grandfather and my grandmother were brother and sister; does that make us kin? One of my favorite foods at schools was apricot halves, I had never had these before. They had a dollop of mayo with grated cheese on top. I had good friends in school, but my best friends were Booty Boy and his family.

After we got electricity in the house, Daddy bought a television. It was a Crosley that was about 15 inches wide, and of course in 1953, it was black and white. It sat on top of a table in Daddy and Mama's bedroom. We were only the second family for miles around to have a TV. Mama, Suzy Mae, and Gertrude would pick beans from the garden all day. At night, they would all sit on the porch, shelling the beans and watching TV through the open window. Mama turned the TV around to face the window. One night, when a band was playing on TV, Gertrude got up and started dancing on the porch. She said she was dancing the Huck-a-Buck. It was wild to watch it. You would think she was possessed by a devil spirit. Daddy gave her a quarter for the show. From then on, he would often give her a quarter to do the Huck-a-Buck.

Booty Boy was always teaching me new things, like the one time he caught a devil's horse. This was a big insect that I learned years later was a praying mantis. I guess he was told this was a devil's horse by the same person who said crayfish were craw devils, crows with split tongues could talk, and headless butterflies would get you a new suit of clothes, and dragon flies were snake doctors.

One of the most amazing feats I ever saw was Booty Boy, Elleck, and Nelson walking on their hands. Almost as good as they were able to walk on their feet. Erba Lee couldn't do it, as hard as he tried because his feet were so large. He could not balance himself upside down. Booty Boy could walk on his hands all over the yard and could even walk up and down steps.

During the tobacco curing season, late summer/early fall, we would put sweet potatoes in the hot coals of the wood flue. These were always good. One season, we had some other colored helping with the tobacco. They had a boy that was a year younger than I. We had found a nest of Japanese hornets in the base of a hollow tree in the edge of the barn lot. We started taking turns running by it while throwing a rock at them. He stumbled and fell right beside the nest. The hornets were all over him. He was stung many time (and messed his britches). That night, Daddy burned out the nest.

Living on a farm, with farm animals having babies all the time, you would think I was aware of where they came from. I had not actually seen a cow, dog, cat, or pig give birth to babies. I didn't see that until I was seven and a half, so when I was around five or six and our cat had five kittens I asked where they came from. I was told she "found" them. I asked where she "found" them and was told "in the woods." At that time, this must have been the pat answer when a child asked adults where babies came from. I was at Granddaddy's (Lee Wilkins's) house shortly after our cat "found" her kittens, and he told me his sow pig was going to "find" baby pigs soon. The next day, I spent several hours walking around in his large hog lot, trying to see if I could find the baby pigs before the sow did. A couple of weeks later, I spent the better part of two days at my home in the woods, trying to "find" puppies. No luck, our dog "found" them the next night.

BEREA

In early 1955 we moved to Berea, to one of the two original Dean home places, this one on Hobgood Road. We lived in an old two-story log house, while our new brick ranch house was being built. Again, we farmed tobacco, had chickens, hogs, cows, and a couple of mules. There was a tenant house on the farm that was built by one of my ancestors in 1922 (the date was on the chimney). There was a colored family that lived in the house. The man helped on the farm, his wife helped Mama with the garden, and their son, Pookie played with me. Pookie had a birth defect, an open hole in his mouth between his left cheek and his jawbone. This hole was clear through and came out in the upper part of his neck, just under his left jaw. As a result, he had a whitish stream of spit (saliva) coming out of the hole and running down his neck, almost all the time. Even when it was not leaking, you could see the trail against his dark skin. This didn't bother Pookie at all. He somehow thought it was special and he had fun with it. He would put some syrup or molasses in his mouth and when it started running out the hole and down his neck, he would lie down on the ground. He then waited for the ants to get on him and follow the stream of sweetness back up through the hole and into his mouth. The hole, being almost half the size of a pencil, kept out large insects. He always spit the ants out and laughed about it.

CUB CREEK

Where we now lived, we had a large creek just below the house and the hog lot. I spent many hours on the creek playing and fishing. The hog lot was just above the creek, and we had two sow pigs in the lot. One of them had given birth to twelve baby pigs and she was huge. In addition to being huge, she was vicious; you dared not get in the pen when she was near. She would come after you, grunting and jaw snapping. Being so big, when she laid down to feed her piglets, she would occasionally mash one to death. When she did that, she would turn around and eat the dead piglet. Daddy was afraid she would get the taste of them, and not wait until they were mashed and dead and just eat them all.

When I left to go to school one day, I heard him talking to Mama about the need to get any dead piglet out of the pen right away. While I was at school, she mashed three of them. Daddy distracted her by putting corn in the lot on the other side. While she was on that side eating, he jumped in the pen and got the three dead babies out. Next, he threw the three dead pigs in the creek to dispose of them. I didn't know any of this, as stated, I was in school. When I got home, I immediately changed clothes and went roaming along the creek. Soon I saw a baby pig, with open eyes, staring up at me from the clear depths of the creek. Then another and another; this is the stuff nightmares are made of. I'll never forget that sight.

The next memory I have here, which will always be with me, was the death of one of our mules. Daddy went to the stable one morning and found old Kate dead. He took our new tractor and chain and dragged old Kate to a part of the farm where we wouldn't be able to smell her when she rotted. Two days later, from the house, you could see dozens of buzzards flying over the area where Kate was. You could see many lit in the trees. At this time, I was eight years old and had always wanted to see a buzzard up real close. So, Saturday morning, I took the .22 caliber rifle to go kill me a buzzard so I could get that close-up look. The buzzards were smart; it's like they knew my intent. When I got within rifle range, they all left before I could get a shot off. I went on over to old dead Kate, holding my nose. She was swollen and I thought I could hear something making a noise inside her. It sounded like a scratching noise. I kicked her and three possums ran out of her butthole. One large possum and two smaller ones. I guess Mama Possum was teaching the little ones about fine cuisine. It's true what they say, a possum will eat anything.

I remember sitting up with Daddy at night when we were curing tobacco. Back then the barns were fired with wood. Wood had to be put in the flue and the barn temperature had to be watched closely to be sure it didn't get too hot or too cold. The fire had to be checked frequently.

It was an all-night job. To get himself awake to check the temperature and fire, he would light a cigarette. Always a Chesterfield, that's what he smoked, no filters then. He would put the lit cigarette between his index and middle finger, then he would go to sleep, laying on the tobacco tying bench. When the cigarette burned down to his fingers and burned them, he woke up and would check the temperature in the barn and the fire in the flue. All during tobacco curing season, he had burned fingers from his makeshift alarm clock.

One night I was with him at the barn and he had the shotgun with him. Someone recently stole some gas out of the tractor that was under the shed next to the barn. He had the gun to put a stop to any new theft. Late that night, while he and I were awake, we heard something walking in the woods near the barn. He raised the gun and yelled out, "I don't know who you are, but you better speak up or I'll shoot you." At that moment, a cow mooed loudly. It was the neighbor's cow that had gotten out of the pasture.

My daddy was not a good man, he drank often. He would sometimes binge drink and be gone for two or three days. One night, Mama and I were alone in the house. Daddy had been gone for two days. Mama knew he was somewhere drunk. Later a man drove Daddy's truck into the yard, he then got out of the truck as a car pulled in. Daddy got out of the car staggering towards the house. The car and the two men drove away, leaving the truck.

Before Daddy could get into the house, Mama grabbed me and pushed me under the bed. She told me to hide there and be quiet. She then ran out the back door and hid in the woods behind the house. You see, when Daddy got drunk, he also got mean. He came into the house cursing and calling for Mama and then calling for me. I kept quiet as I saw him walk by the bed. He looked all over the house for us. Then I heard a shotgun blast in the next room. He thought Mama was hiding behind an open door, between it and the wall. The blast blew a hole in the door and destroyed a table lamp that was on a table behind the door. He then got angrier and was yelling my name and Mama's. Next, I heard him go outside looking for us.

A few minutes later, I heard Mama scream and a shotgun blast. I thought he had killed her, and I started crying. He came back into the house and I tried my best to stifle my crying so he wouldn't hear me under the bed and shoot me too. I heard him lay down on the couch in the next room. He went to sleep or passed out; I could hear him snoring. I slipped out from under the bed and out of the house. When I got outside, Mama was coming out of the woods. She had not been shot. He must have shot at a tree or shadow, thinking it was her. We got into the truck, both crying, and went to my grandmother's house, my mama's Mama. We stayed there two days and nights before returning home; after he came to Grandmother's house and said he was sorry for what he had done.

Daddy had always loved to hunt, and he had started taking me with him quail hunting. I had no gun; I was just along to learn. We had a brown and white German, short haired, pointer named Brownie. He was a great bird dog that we had for many years. This dog loved to hunt but had gotten so old that he tired quickly, and couldn't get across downed trees, gullies, or creeks. When we came to them, Daddy would pick him up and carry him across. He so loved to hunt that if you left the door open to the pickup truck, he would manage to get inside and sit on the seat and wait there, ready to go find birds.

THE NEW HOUSE

Our new ranch-style brick home was finished late in 1956. This was a huge modern home with eight rooms, a large kitchen, dining room, and living room. It had all hardwood floors, a utility room with a large sink, a back porch with a sink and three bedrooms. The house had twelve closets and a large screened porch on the end. It was the newest most modern house around at that time. I had my own bedroom with a closet and a separate toy closet. We moved into the house; it was wonderful.

Up until this time whenever I did something wrong, Daddy punished me with a switch or small limb he broke off a bush. These beatings were always painful and

I cried. Maybe, because I was now older or bigger, the punishment now was with his leather belt and it hurt.

A neighbor probably saved my life one day. We had not been in the new house very long maybe two months when I was up in the attic just exploring. I was directly above my bedroom when I stepped off the flooring onto the Celotex ceiling tile. None of it broke but several pieces came loose and were hanging down into the ceiling of my bedroom. The neighbor, Wallace Blalock Jr. came by to see Daddy about something farm related. He saw me setting on the steps at the back door crying. Crying because I just knew I was going to be killed, beaten to death. I told him Daddy was not there and had left early that morning. He could see that I was very upset and asked what was wrong. I told him what had happened, and he said let's go have a look at it. He saw it and asked me to find some long straight pins or needles. I found several, and he pushed the tiles, 12 inches x 18 inches back together and pinned them. When finished you could not even see that they had ever been loose. I was very thankful to him that I was going to live.

GOODBYE DADDY

One morning in January 1957, I was eating breakfast in the kitchen before going to school. Mama had already gone to work at John Umstead Hospital. Daddy came in and said he was going to Durham. I spoke up and said, "Goodbye, Daddy." That was the only time I ever in my life told him goodbye. Later that evening, about 7:00 P.M. a man rang the doorbell to the front door. Mama and I were there in the house. Mama went to the door and the man said Daddy had a wreck and was in the hospital. We got in our car and drove to the hospital in Durham. We were told Daddy was in a coma and they had to remove part of his skull because of brain swelling. He never regained consciousness and died. The truck that he was driving when he wrecked, was not damaged except for its back glass was broken out. The thought at the time, was that he had been thrown out of the truck and may have slid down the highway or may have somehow been dragged down the highway. His whole right side had friction burns even the side sole of his right shoe. The truck was actually driven back to our house and sat there in the yard.

It was the custom at the time, to bring the deceased back to the house to lie in casket, with it open, so that family and friends could view the departed. This was done, and for two days after Daddy was brought to the house, Brownie (Daddy's bird dog) sat on the back door steps and howled. First it was almost continuous, then on the second day, he still sat there and would howl every once in a while. During those two days, he ate nothing, just drank water from a bowl beside the step. He knew his master was gone. Daddy was taken to the church and buried after two days at home. At that time, it was the largest attended funeral ever at the church.

Daddy was well liked in the community; people regarded him with respect. Those people only knew one side of him. They didn't see the other side that Mama and I did.

Later, the truck was repaired and brought back to the house. Brownie never got near the truck again for the rest of his days. He died a year later. He had lost his hearing completely. When it was feeding time, you had to go find him and show him the food. He then would follow you until you sat the bowl down, and he would eat. One day after school, I fixed a bowl of food for him and went to find him. He was in the old chicken house; in a section we had no chickens in and the door was always left open for him to use as his place. He followed me and the food back to the house, in the backyard where I put it down for him. Later, I looked out the window and saw him lying beside his food bowl. The way he was lying, I knew he was dead. I went outside and hugged him. With my first thought that he was now in Heaven, bird hunting with Daddy. Then I quickly realized that only Brownie would be in Heaven, not Daddy.

Several months later, Mama, Daddy's sister my Aunt Ruth, and I went to Florida for a vacation. We went to Daytona Beach where all but me got severely sunburned. I stayed in the water, they lay on the beach. Their burns were so bad they had to go to the emergency room of the nearest hospital. They could only wear nightgowns, everything else hurt too much. We stopped at Silver Springs on the way back to go on the glass-bottom-boat rides. They still felt too bad and sat on picnic tables while I did go on the boat ride.

At the time, 1957, you could buy a live alligator for five dollars. Mama bought me one that was about twelve inches long. When we got home, I put him in a wire cage that was kept in the large utility room sink. Over the next several months he grew from the raw hamburger I fed him. By winter he was 24 inches long. I came home from school one day, and he was not in his cage. I looked for him all over the house. When Mama got home from work, she helped look. We found him behind the chest freezer in the utility room. Mama said I could not keep him in the house anymore, and he was moved to the back porch, which was screened in. Two nights later he froze to death. I was sad, but not too much so, because he had bitten me several times. That next day, Saturday, I took his lifeless body down the hill, down the road next to the bridge over Cub Creek. I lay him on the shoulder of the road as if he had just crawled out of the creek. I sat in the woods where I could watch unseen. A short time later a Mr. Buck Morris came driving down the road in his pickup. Mr. Morris actually had a wooden peg leg. He braked his truck and got out about 30 from the alligator. He stared picking up rocks and throwing them at the dead alligator. Of course, the gator didn't move even when hit. Mr. Morris realized or at least thought he was dead, so he started toward him, lost his balance and pivoted around in a circle on his peg leg three times, regained his balance and walked to the gator. He nudged at it with his peg leg then reached down ever so carefully and picked him up by his tail. He put the gator in his truck bed and drove to Berea where he nailed him up on the back of a store that was run by Mr. Collie Jones. Word got around and people came from miles around to see the 2 ft. alligator that came out of Cub Creek.

Mr. William Jones was the county 4-H Director. He was also the same William Jones that had POWs working on his farm during the war. Not long after Daddy died, Mr. Jones asked me at the church one Sunday if I would like to raise a calf for a 4-H project to show at the State Fair. We talked to Mama and she said okay. Within two weeks, I had a Holstein Calf that had to be bottle fed. I raised the calf to be one of the biggest and best pets I ever had. Mr. Jones often came by to see the progress and to give encouragement. I named the calf Babe, you know, "Babe the Blue Ox." When I was outside, she followed me everywhere. I would often go into the woods and hide; she could always find me. At that time, I had several rabbit boxes set in the woods to catch rabbits. I would check them all every morning before going to school. Babe went with me every morning. She actually followed me into the house several times until Mama said not ever again. I did take her to the State Fair, and she won a blue ribbon and was sadly sold by auction at the fair's end. Mr. Jones was very helpful in all of this and in keeping me interested in 4-H so much so that I went to all the meetings and to summer camp several summers. He stepped in when Daddy was gone and seemed to realize I needed something to keep me busy and to be responsible for. It worked and I will always be grateful to him.

Mama remarried in 1959; his name was Harman Bodgardner, and he was from the edge of the mountains of North Carolina, the town of Conover. He worked at John Umstead State Mental Hospital in Butner, as Mama did. If ever there was a good stepfather, it was he. I soon called him Daddy. When in Butner before he met Mama, he was a scout master and that was one of the things he brought to Berea. He started the Boy and Cub Scouts here by getting two charter numbers from the Boy Scout Council. After starting it and making sure it was on a good footing, he stepped aside and let others take over. He was a good father to me. He worked full-time at John Umstead and on the farm raising Black Angus cattle. He was always there to give me good advice and support. I didn't regard him as a stepfather, but a father in every sense of the word, and he never laid a hand on me. He used reason and common sense to guide, not physical threats.

The next six years were typical, living in the rural south and on a farm. There was plenty of hard work raising black angus cattle, the corn to make corn sileage to feed them and taking care of the pastures. I stayed busy as a Boy Scout going to meetings, camping out and going to the Scout Jamboree. As a member of the 4-H Club, I went to these meetings and camp. I played and lettered in both basketball and baseball in high school. Our school had no football program. There were fistfights, skipping school, starting to smoke, several girlfriends, and a prom with a much older girl.

In 1963, I completed the 10th grade of high school at Berea, North Carolina, the same school my mother and father had graduated from. That summer, I worked in tobacco for my two uncles, Archie and Brindell. Archie the "Double A Whistler" and Thelma raised tobacco on a farm beside and with his Father Lee, my grandfather. They now had two children, a son and daughter. Archie was also a full-time deputy sheriff. Brindell and his wife were also full-time tobacco farmers on their farm just outside Oxford. They had three daughters and a son. Eventually, I worked at Hillman Currin's Esso, pumping gas and later in construction building a wing onto the hospital where I was born, in Oxford.

On November 18th, the day after my seventeenth birthday, I enlisted in the US Army. Since I was underage, not yet eighteen, my mother had to give written permission for me to enlist. 1 went through basic training at Fort Jackson, South Carolina, and then advanced infantry training at Fort Gordon, Georgia.

1964

While at Fort Gordon, Georgia, a fellow Army buddy and I came up with the idea to start going to local family reunions to get home- cooked food instead of the swill the Army fed us. We started checking the local newspaper for family reunion announcements. These were always on the week-ends, and we usually were off duty with weekend passes. We would go in civilian clothes, walk around introducing ourselves as cousin so and so and the other was a friend. This worked great for many weeks. We did finally stop this when we went to the Harris Reunion. You see, my buddy and I are Caucasian (white) and the Harris family was Africa American (black). We quickly left without saying we were cousin to anyone.

After completing training at Fort Gordon and breaking bread with so many "new relatives," I went home on leave for a week.

I had received orders to travel to Fort Dix, New Jersey and await a flight from McGuire Air Force Base, which was across the road from Fort Dix. The flight would be to Berlin, Germany. The orders said I would have a tour of duty in Berlin of just over two years. I was excited about it. I had heard that duty in Germany, especially Berlin, was good. I was somewhat apprehensive about the whole Berlin Wall situation.

When I got home on leave, Mama acted a little unusual, this had started when I called her from Fort Gordon and first told her about my orders to Berlin, Germany. On the phone call she immediately fell silent and only spoke again when I said I'll call you later, when I find out when my bus gets to Oxford. It was a curt okay. I thought it was because of all the things in the news about people getting killed crossing over, under, and through the Berlin wall. This unusual behavior continued all week and had gotten worse. She just wasn't hardly talking to anyone.

My bus to Fort Dix was scheduled for Saturday. Mama took Friday, the day before, off from work. She told Daddy she needed to stay home to spend some time with me and help me pack. Helping me pack was of course not necessary. All I had were my military uniforms and shaving kit with toothbrush. This made me wonder.

We sat having lunch "dunna" at the kitchen table. The table where family decisions were made and serious discussions were had.

Mama started out by saying she had something to tell me that she had never told anyone before. She then told me about Hans Krause, about him being a POW who had worked on the farm along with another named Werner Tobler. She talked about how helpful and respectful they were. I reminded her that I had heard the story of the Double A Whistler, Uncle Archie, shooting the Nazi sniper and he ended up at the family farm. So, I know about the POWs. She then dropped the bomb telling me that she had fallen in love with Hans and she thought he had with her. Then she said Hans is your father, not Wilson. At first, I thought she was just kidding me but I saw something in her attitude and body language that I had never seen before. I couldn't speak while my brain was trying to process what she had just told me.

I could only ask her, "Are you certain?"

"Yes," she said, "and as I said, no one knows about this. I never even told my two closest friends, Maude or Mary Elizabeth." She said she never had the intention of telling me this, but it was the right thing to do and this was the right time. Mama said maybe Hans's feelings for her had saved all their lives because some men would have reacted with vengeance. Vengeance and hatred when they found out that a family member was the one responsible for their being shot, captured and being held as a POW. Some men would have gone into a rage and tried to kill them all.

She said to me, "Don't you remember all the remarks from friends and relatives over the years saying how much you looked like me and so little like Wilson?" I thought, Yes, I've heard that many times but never before had any reason to wonder about or question it. Liss even asked me once years ago if I was "'dopted." She said that even Wilson had commented more than once how little you looked like him.

I asked again, "Are you sure?"

Again, she said "Yes." She said I was born eight months after Wilson got home from the war and everyone just thought you came a month early. She said my birth was almost exactly nine months after she and Hans had shared "carnal knowledge." I asked if it was rape, and she said certainly not.

She said she had never heard from him since he left the farm, so she didn't even know if he was still alive or not. She said of course he doesn't know about you; doesn't know he has a son.

She then told me his story, about his Uncle and Aunt's farm in Pertz, Germany, near Berlin. About his mother and father, my real grandparents, who did live in Berlin.

I told Mama to just stop for a while; I had to go outside, clear my head, and walk around some. I did this, went out into the yard where I walked around. I walked down the hill towards the creek, then out into one of the pastures. The whole time I had this feeling of being alone, like I really wasn't a part of the Dean family I had known all my life. It seemed that everyone and everything was a stranger to me, it was a terrible and frightening feeling.

I went back into the house where she was waiting for me. She said she was sorry about this and that she had never planned to tell me about Hans. She said when she found out I had orders to go to Germany, she realized that she had to tell me. She had to so that I could know about my real father and find him while I was there if I wanted to. This, she knew was the right time for me to know.

She then showed me a photo of Hans and Werner. She had kept this hidden away all these years since 1946. Once, when Harman came across the photo, she just told him they were the two POWs that had worked on her father's farm. He had heard some things about them over the years but certainly not about a love affair. Even in this old photo, I could see the resemblance I had to Hans.

She then showed me the old copper coin dated 1785 and told me that it was supposed to be a good luck coin given Hans by his grandfather. She also told me about how often the coin had been found by the authorities when Hans was searched.

How they always laughed at him and let him keep it when he said it was his good luck coin. She gave me the coin and the photo which I later decided to put in my suitcase for the trip overseas.

The rest of that day and evening I was in deep thought and didn't have much to say. Harman later commented, and I told him I was just a little apprehensive about going to Berlin since things there were unsettled and tense. Of course, Mama knew why I was quiet. Saturday morning, we had breakfast, then went to Oxford for me to catch my dog "Greyhound" bus to New Jersey. As we said our goodbyes, Mama whispered in my ear that she was sorry, she loved me, and good luck.

On the long bus ride, I just stewed, was not interested in the sights at all. I finally made the decision to put the whole thing in the back of my mind and ignore it, pretend I didn't know.

An elderly lady sitting across the aisle from me said, "I see by your uniform you are in the Army. I have a grandson in the Army, his name is Pvt. Thomas Sherman, do you know him?"

I answered with respect, "No, Ma'am, I don't." What I really wanted to say was, there are

420,000 men in the Army, why would you think I would know him? At the same time, I remembered the almost impossible odds of the Double A Whistler shooting the sniper who ended up on the farm Archie grew up on and him, that sniper being my father, so yeah, maybe I could know her grandson, but I don't.

While briefly stationed at Fort Dix, New Jersey, I went AWOL. Back then, you stayed at Fort Dix, which was right across from McGuire Air Force Base. You stayed there sometimes weeks waiting for your flight out of McGuire to take you to Europe. While at Fort Dix, you often pulled K.P. (Kitchen Police) duty. This was always scheduled and posted ahead on a bulletin board, so you knew when you were detailed to work and when you were off. My bunkmate was from Washington, DC, not too far away. We came up with the idea of going to Washington DC for the weekend since we were off. 1 would go to my aunt's in Maryland, just outside of DC. Neither John (my bunkmate) nor I had a car. We set out thumbing from Fort Dix to DC in our Class A Greens. We had walked about three miles and John asked what my MOS (Military Occupational Specialty) job was. I told him it was 11 B10, infantry. I asked him what his was, and he said Military Police. So here we were AWOL (away without leave) together and he was a military cop. We caught rides to DC and went our separate ways. I caught a dog 'Greyhound" back to Fort Dix Sunday night. John was already back. We were never missed. I shipped out two days later, and never saw John again.

When I got to Berlin, I was assigned to the 2nd Squad, 3rd Platoon of Company B, 4th BN, 18th Infantry Division.

I was so busy there I had no time to think about what Mama had revealed to me, and furthermore I did not want to. I reaffirmed what I had decided on the bus, ignore it, it didn't happen!

PFC Tuttrow was in the same squad as I at McNair Barracks in Berlin, Germany. He was a strange guy. I don't know how he made it through basic and advanced infantry training. He was a person who lived with a fixed routine, maybe he was OCD. He had to stay in the shower for exactly seventeen minutes every day. He had to spend exactly the same amount of time brushing his teeth. Once there was a fire drill. Everyone was out of the barracks but him. He said he couldn't go out of the building until he put up all his laundry. As time went on, it was clear he couldn't continue to cope with military life. McNair Barracks was a three-story building. One day, PFC Tuttrow ran into the First Sergeant's office and shouted that someone was on top of the building (flat roof), going to jump off. He immediately ran up the steps to the top of the building. When the First Sergeant went outside and looked up to the rooftop, there was Tuttrow. He was finally talked down and was sent home and discharged.

PFC Gomez was from Puerto Rico. He had a very neatly trimmed mustache. He was lean and good-looking. His only problem was that he was a drunk who frequently went out drinking in the clubs in downtown Berlin. Somehow, he always made it back to the barracks, where he usually passed out. Unfortunately for the rest of this squad, he would be so hungover he would often miss reveille in the early morning. Another issue was when he came into the facility drunk at night, he would get into arguments or fights with anyone.

He was written up for these deeds and sometimes charged with an Article 14, as a formal punishment that stayed on his record. At that time in the military, when one soldier in the squad broke the rules, everyone in the squad was punished. This punishment varied from extra duty for all, restriction to the barracks, five-mile runs, extra punitive training, loss of PX (Post Exchange) privilege, etc. No amount of threatening or sometimes fights with Gomez changed his behavior.

We all continued to be penalized for his misbehavior. The following deeds were done to Gomez by other members of the squad to hopefully make him behave.

He came in drunk and passed out. While he was out, exactly half of that perfectly groomed mustache was shaved off. The next morning, he was in a rage, but had to shave off the other half himself.

Several nights later he came in and passed out, and while out, his single bunk with him in it was taken to the shower room. The shower room was large, about 12' by 14' with numerous showerheads protruding from the wall. His bunk, with him in it, was put under three showerheads and all three were cut on with cold water. He actually lay there for about fifteen minutes getting soaked before he woke up. He was still so drunk; he could not comprehend what had happened to him.

For several weeks, he stayed sober and tried to walk the line. His good behavior did not continue. He screwed up and the entire squad had to pay the price.

The next time he came in drunk raising hell and then passed out, his life was put in danger. While passed out, a mattress cover was pulled off a mattress. The mattress covers were actually large cloth bags with one end open with tie-strings so that the mattress would be placed in it and it would be tied up. He was put in the empty mattress cover, then hung out the 3rd story window of the squad room. Those strings at the end were tied to the steam pipes that went to the radiators, inside under the windows. When he awoke, he started yelling and kicking, not realizing that he could break the strings and fall. He yelled so much and so loudly that an officer walking by underneath saw and heard him. He went into the building and he and several other NCOs came running up to the third floor, into the room and pulled Gomez back inside. The entire squad was punished for this. The next three mornings we had to get up at 3:00 A.M. and go for a six-mile run in full combat gear. In retrospect, if the strings had torn, and he fell onto the concrete, he would have certainly died.

After this, PFC Gomez actually started acting much worse. He continued to get into fights, never passed inspections, and caused us all much grief. The next time he came in drunk and passed out was a Friday night. Several of the squad members got him up while he was, of course, still fully dressed. They removed his dog tags, his military ID card and all other documents that would identify him. With a squad member supporting him on either side, and two more to help, he was taken to the nearest S Bahn train depot. Back then you could get on this train similar to a subway and go into East Berlin past the Berlin Wall. The East Germans and Russians controlled East Berlin. The only problem was you <u>could not come back out of East Berlin</u>. Being drunk and with no ID, it took the State Department three weeks to get PFC Gomez released from behind the wall. He was then sent home with a dishonorable discharge. This solved the squad's problems.

Outside West Berlin was a large forest called the Grunewald. The battalion often spent weeks there on military maneuvers, practicing for war in the woods. This was a beautiful place. We dug foxholes and ate C-rations. We did not build fires for fear they might get out of control. The forest was also filled with wild boar. When we saw them during the day, we shot blanks at them, and they went away. One night about 2:00 A.M., the whole platoon was awakened by someone screaming and yelling. One of our members of the third platoon was on his way to the latrine to relieve himself when a wild boar ran him up a tree. It was then pawing the ground and charging the tree. Several platoon members fired blanks, and he went away.

Early in the year, the whole battalion went by convoy to a place in West Germany called Wild Flicken. We went there to practice war. This was a beautiful part of West Germany. There was also a large monastery there filled with Catholic Monks. The monks supported the monastery by making and selling beer and beer steins (mugs). It just seemed odd to me to have a brewery to make beer, a beer hall next to it in which to drink the beer, and a chapel between the two to pray in. The oddity to me, is in part because I grew up a Baptist in the South, where beer and church don't mix. I did sample the wares and bought two one-litre steins that I still have.

Spandau Prison in Berlin was a place where Nazi-convicted war criminals were housed. There were only three inmates housed there in the entire prison. They were Von Schirach, Speer, and Hess. They were sentenced to life. The first two, Von Schirach and Speer got along fine. They did not associate with Hess. The four powers: French, American, British, and Russian took turns guarding the prisoners. Each nation had duty three months at a time. When the Americans had it, the job was done by the 4th Battalion, 18th Infantry. This was rotated between each company and platoons in the battalion. I stood on the top of the 20ft prison wall and walked the parapet for eight hours at a time when it rotated to my platoon and company. Hess would see the other two inmates in the outside courtyard during the day and would make insulting comments to them and actually bark at them like a dog. This was an interesting duty, guarding these notorious war criminals.

Later, I was chosen to work on the Berlin Honor Guard. This new job was at Brigade Headquarters. This job also included a drill team that I was selected for. This was a very prestigious job, and I enjoyed it. Two weeks later, I was told that the Honor Guard 2nd in command, a first Lt. William Averette wanted to see me in his office right away. I was somewhat concerned because normally no one is called into his office unless they have done something wrong and are going to be disciplined in some way. This was usually one of three things, either being sent back to their infantry unit, an Article 15, or a Court Martial. In searching my memory, I could not figure out what I had done wrong.

After the salute, he told me to sit down. He asked if I knew what (ACA) was. I said I knew a little about it from others in the Honor Guard, but I had not talked with anyone that had actually worked there. He said we are considering reassigning you to ACA, but first you must have a Secret Clearance. He said someone from a branch of the Army Security Agency (ASA) will come here to interview you and start the process, which is an investigation regarding your past. They will meet with you in three weeks and conduct a polygraph (lie detector) test. In the meantime, you need to get information from back home that will speed up this process. He said, "I see from your 201 File that you were a Boy Scout, an Explorer Scout, and a member of the 4H Club additionally, you went to two different schools." I answered, yes sir. "You need to get the addresses of the schools, the years enrolled there, and the entry and exit dates of the scouts and 4H club and where they were chartered. The addresses of the places you have lived and when you lived there, is also needed." I asked the lieutenant if me putting a live black snake in my third grade teacher's, Mrs. Triplete's, desk drawer would disqualify me from working at ACA. He asked if she died from it or was injured, no, was the answer. He laughed and said that would be up to the investigator.

That night I wrote Mama and asked her to get the Scout information from my stepfather and to also write down the other information and please send it to me right away.

While waiting for this information to be sent I continued with my duties there at Brigade Headquarters. It wasn't work all the time; we had card and pool tables in the Day Room. I was friends with another North Carolinian from Kinston. We were both good at shooting pool, and we picked up extra spending money, playing against other members of the Honor Guard.

Three weeks later, I met with the investigator, from ASA, a Sergeant First Class Malcolm Obrian. I had received the requested information from Mama.

The interview and lie detector test took five hours; it was very grueling. At the conclusion I was told that they would have to check and verify all the information I had given him, but he did not think there would be a problem with me getting the needed clearance to work at ACA. I did not ask him about the liability of the snake in the drawer.

Since I had been stationed in Berlin, Mama and I had exchanged numerous letters. She never pushed the issue about Hans in all her letters. I could only assume that she was all right with whatever decision I made in his regard. Just once, she asked in a letter if I had yet been down to the farming area south of Berlin.

In a few months, I was notified that the Secret Clearance had been approved, and I was promoted to Corporal E-4 and then assigned to the best job in Berlin. It was security for the Allied Control Authority (ACA). This was a beautiful building, three stories overlooking a city park. It had a large second floor porch that Hitler used to stand on and make speeches. Only about a quarter of the building was used to control the flight paths into Berlin's Templehoff Airport. Berlin itself was divided into four sections, one for each of the four powers. Since East Berlin was behind the wall that was all the way through the city, all air flights were tightly restricted because the Russians forbid any flights over their sector of the city or East Germany, which they controlled. The rooms these people worked in on the second floor were filled with radar screens and communication equipment. It was a very busy place with constant talk via radio to pilots, copilots and flight engineers. Russians, French, British, and Americans all worked here together or at least in the same room.

The predominant language used was English, but I was told that on every shift there was an American that spoke and understood Russian and

French. The Honor Guard, ACA, was in charge of security, and there were living quarters on the first floor near the front entrance for us. The function of ACA was a twenty-four-hour, seven-day-a-week job. This was not only for French, British, Russian, and Americans, but also those of us Army personnel who manned the security posts of the building. There were three people for each of the four powers and for each shift. There was always a non-commissioned officer, a sergeant who was the driver, a lieutenant and a full bird colonel or a lieutenant colonel. We had to salute the officers in each car that came in and those going out when the shift changed. Occasionally, the outgoing car had to stop at the entrance/exit onto the street to let other vehicle traffic get past before it could get out. There was a new three-story apartment building being built just down the street and many vehicles, especially large trucks were constantly coming by. This slowed the exit from ACA. When this happened, often the occupants of the exit vehicle would chat with whomever of us was on duty at the time. The Russians would not chat, with one exception.

The exception was a Russian colonel that worked the day shift. He was the only Russian that would talk to any of us American Servicemen, and they all spoke English.

He was friendly in his conversation, asking us where we were from in the US, how long we had been stationed in Berlin, and if we had yet been to Vietnam, etc. His name was Colonel Drowbeski. Over a period of time, he came to know each of us by our rank and name and addressed us in that manner. The French, British and, of course, our own American Servicemen were all cordial and would chat while waiting to drive out.

The puzzling thing to me was that this Russian colonel was the only one that ever threw trash, crumpled up cigarette packs, or paper out the car window. He didn't do this every day, but at least twice weekly. It seemed to me that he was trying to hide it from the other occupants of the car. I thought maybe he is ashamed of his littering, maybe it's a compulsion that he can't control. Whenever this happened someone would always come walking by within the hour and pick up the litter. It was always one of three people. My thoughts were that they must live nearby and just want to keep the area clean. I even spoke to a gentleman one day after he picked up a crumpled wad of paper. By now I could speak and understand German fairly well. He said he just wanted to keep the place looking good. Germans and Swiss do not litter; their countries and cities are litter free. I'm sure the colonel knew this; it would be obvious to anyone who lived or worked in these countries. So why did he keep throwing trash out the car window? This looked habitual, and it made me suspicious. I talked to my coworkers and they had seen the same activity with this colonel and the same three who came by to pick up the trash. I decided to go up the chain of command with my suspicions and informed the guard commander, Captain Mark Currin.

Four days later, a man in civilian clothes came to our assembly room accompanied by Captain Mark Currin. We were questioned about what several of us had observed. We were ordered to ignore it and not to discuss it with anyone.

While at the ACA and not on duty, I frequently walked around in this beautiful cavernous building. So much beautiful architecture, so many rooms unused since the war. Some of the rooms still had some furniture in them. I often went out on the balcony overlooking the park where Hitler had given many of his speeches. I stood in the same spot he had stood in taking in the beauty of the park below. This was a great place to see, think and reflect. As a result, I came to a decision. I knew that within eight months I would be rotating back to the States, and I came to the realization that I had to face reality. I knew if I didn't find Hans or at least try to, that 1 would certainly someday regret it. I even thought about someday my children may ask who their grandparents are, and I needed to be able to tell them all the truth, not just part of it.

I had no idea about how to begin this hunt. When off duty two days later, I went to the Office of Administrative Information in the Berlin Capital Building. I spoke to someone there at reception, and they had someone escort me to the Office of Military Data pre 1948. A young lady by the name of Betsy Ann Hoyer spoke with me. She spoke English without hardly any accent. She was suspicious when I asked about former POWs. She quizzed me about why I wanted information on former POW Hans Krause. She stated later that part of her job was to protect any information about former POWs in case someone had a score to settle with them about something they may have done years earlier. I assured her I had no vendetta in mind but that he was my father that I never knew about until a year and a half ago. I wanted to find him and learn all the things about him and the family that I never knew. I told her all I knew, about the farm in Pertz, his sister, his parents in Berlin and showed her the photo. She said she would help me but that it would take some time. She asked if I could come back to her office in three days. We made an appointment for three days later for a time when I was off duty. Needless to say, the next three days were filled with excitement, but some dread.

When I got to her office three days later, she told me, "Your father is alive." She had contacted the office of the mayor in Pertz, and they had pulled up the district information. Hans still lived on the farm, now his. She had not told them why she needed the information, but they had given her the address, which she gave to me. She was excited about this upcoming reunion and made me promise to come back and tell her all about it later.

I requested five days leave time to begin the next Tuesday. That night, I wrote Mama a letter using very cryptic language in it such as, "I'm taking a few days off to see a beautiful tourist and farming area named Pertz, not too far from Berlin."

I packed some uniform clothes, toiletries, the photo, and coin. I caught the train the next morning. It was a short one-hour ride to Pertz. I checked into the only hotel in town and found a taxi to take me out to the farm. The ride was full of intense feelings some of dread, some of excitement and joy. We got to the farm; he drove me right up to the front door. I asked the driver to just wait a while for me, in case this was a mistake, and he asked no questions. I paid him.

I knocked on the door, it was quickly opened by a man that I immediately knew was my father. This is the image I had seen in the mirror for so many years. He looked at me quizzically and asked what I wanted. I asked if I could come in. I had worn my dress green uniform thinking it might open doors for me. He said yes. We went inside after I waved off the taxi driver. He offered me a seat and the conversation began.

I asked him if he remembered the man that shot him in France. He hesitated, then said yes and said they called him the Double A Whistler. He asked if I knew him, I said yes, he is my Uncle. I then asked him if he remembered Mary and Lee Wilkins, their other son Brindell and daughter Marilee. He said yes, and I then told him that Marilee was my mother and that he was my father. He turned white as in shock, then he put his face in his hands and began to sob. This went on for several minutes. I felt compelled to get up and walk over to him. He stood up immediately, reached out his hand to shake mine, immediately drew it back and wrapped his arms around me in the most heartfelt hug I've ever had. This hug went on for several minutes along with his sobs. This brought tears to my eyes as well. I then showed him the photo of he and Werner that Brindell had taken and then the 1785 coin that I took out of my pocket. When I gave it to him, he started to sob again.

After a couple of hours, we both regained our composure. He wanted to know all about Mama and the rest of the family. We talked for hours. He said he could clearly see the resemblance between us and saw it when he first spotted me on the porch. He talked at great length about his work there on my grandfather's farm when he was a POW, about the sad death of Old John, about my grandmother's cooking. He talked about what he found when he returned to Germany, the devastation especially in Berlin. His father was killed after the war in an accident during reconstruction.

When working to clean up debris from a bombed out, building, part of a wall fell and crushed him. His mother, my grandmother, was still alive living with his sister and her husband in Berlin. He said I had to see them; they were my family.

Later, I told him I was staying in a hotel in Pertz and would need to call a taxi to come get me and return to Pertz. He said absolutely not, you are my son; you must stay here with me. We have a lot to catch up on. We rode his truck into town to the hotel. I got my stuff and checked out. Back to the farm we went where he prepared a wonderful meal. Afterwards, we sat and talked until neither of us could stay awake any longer. We said good night, and I went off to the room he had shown me earlier.

The next morning, we talked at breakfast, he said he had been married but his wife had died five years earlier. That they never had children, so I was a blessing, his only child. He said he had loved my mother so very much and when he had to leave her his heart was broken. For years he lived with his aunt and uncle as nearly a hermit until his sister and her husband finally got him out of his shell and introduced him to the woman that he married. His aunt and uncle had both passed away several years ago, leaving him this farm as they had promised. I asked what had happened to his aunt and uncle. He said his uncle had finally been killed by his asthma. Shortly after the war while Hans was there on the farm, his uncle had an attack that was so severe that it caused his heart to stop. His aunt died about eighteen months later from an unknown illness, probably cancer.

Later we walked over the whole farm. He showed me his corn, barley, and wheat fields. He had chickens, cows, and hogs, all very similar to what I had been used to my whole life, but no tobacco. It wasn't so much of a farm to make a lot of money; it was mainly to sustain his life.

He talked about how he had subscribed to the Nazi philosophy and lies. About how he had become disillusioned when he had seen all the newspaper accounts of treatment the Nazis had carried out against Jews, American POWs, and others while he was a POW. He said he had been lucky. Maybe it was the coin. He had lived, lived well in captivity, had fallen in love, and has a son.

He asked about Wilson, Mama's first husband and about Harman, my stepfather. He was dismayed when I told him about some of Wilson's deeds. He said the idea crossed his mind to return to North Carolina, to see Mama but of course he didn't because of her already being married to Wilson, and he was sure she had gotten on with her life. He said that he would have returned if he had known about me. I told him Mama said she had told no one about their hayloft love affair, and I only knew about it and him just before I shipped out to Berlin.

Later that day, a car drove up as he and I sat on the front porch talking. Three people got out: an elderly woman and a younger man and woman. Hans introduced them; it was very moving the way he made the introductions.

"My son Jerry, this is your grandmother, my mother Helga." She reached out to take my hand and then instead hugged me as we both teared up. He next said again with much emphasis, "My son Jerry, this is your aunt, my sister Grettle and her husband Gerhard." She hugged me and Gerhard and I shook hands. When I saw Gerhard "my newfound Uncle," I recognized him as one of the people that I had seen walking by ACA and picking up trash. That trash being paper crumpled up and crushed cigarette packs that were thrown out by the Russian colonel. This intrigued me, and I wondered if he recognized me. It also made me a little guarded towards him.

Their coming was a surprise to me. Hans said he had called them the night before and told them about me and insisted they come visit. They stayed until late in the day, and we drove into Pertz for supper. Our discussions never stopped. They wanted to know all about my family back in North Carolina, about our farm there, what everyday life was like and, of course, all about me, their newfound relative. They wanted to know what my Army job in Berlin was. Grettle gave me their Berlin address and said that I had to visit them since their house was right there in the city limits. In fact, I knew the street they lived on; it was only about sixteen city blocks from the ACA building where my duty station was.

After supper we drove back to the farm, said our goodbyes with hugs, and again a handshake with Gerhard. They left heading back to the city.

My daddy, Hans, and I stayed up talking late into the night again and then to bed.

After breakfast the next morning, we drove into town to pick up things needed on the farm and then to a church. Daddy wanted me to see the grave of his father, my grandfather. He said it is sad you never knew him or he you. I agreed, then asked why he was buried here in Pertz instead of Berlin where he lived. He said that there was so much destruction in Berlin including the cemeteries that he, his mother, and sister decided to bury him here, at the church he attended. Pertz was far more peaceful and sustained little damage during the war. Since he attended this church, he would care for the grave. The rest of the day and night, before bed, was filled with conversation and a lot of speculation, such as "what ifs."

The next morning after breakfast, and after feeding the farm animals he took me back to town so I could catch the train back to Berlin. We hugged and made a promise to see each other again soon.

Three weeks later, on Friday evening after I got off duty, I caught a cab to my Aunt Grettle's house sixteen blocks away. The house was not special but was neat in appearance as those around it were.

Hans had arrived earlier in the day by train from Pertz and then a cab to the house as I did. Grettle and my grandmother were preparing a meal while Gerhard, my father, and I sat in their living room and talked. We talked about how

West Berlin had recovered from the war to the point that you could not see any remaining damage anywhere. At the same time, East Berlin, on the other side of the wall had very little reconstruction and in many areas looked as it did at the end of the war in 1946. This, of course, was due to occupation by the Russians and their heavy-handed rule. I told them about more than one instance when I had been with Army buddies in a bar having drinks just a few feet from the wall and heard screams and shots.

This happened frequently due to the desolation, unemployment, and lack of freedom under Russian and East German border guards. The people in the East knew how normal life was now in West Berlin and they wanted to be on this side of the wall and many were killed trying to get here. Gerhard talked a little about his time as a Nazi soldier. His comments were general without any details or specifics. It was as though he was ashamed or secretive about his time in the Nazi military. I was a guest in their house, so I didn't push the issue to get him to reveal more. He changed the subject, going back to our earlier discussion saying he had relatives, a cousin and aunt and uncle living on the other side of the wall. He had had one cousin who was shot and killed trying to cross over. Still, I didn't let him know that I recognized him and as far as I could tell he did not recognize me.

It continued to amaze me that everyone in this household spoke English so well, except my grandmother. Often my daddy had to translate for her. When I commented about it, he said that he, his sister, and Gerhard were taught English in school, and my grandmother's generation was not. Since the war she had learned quite a bit from casual contact with Americans and Grettle had been teaching her.

We sat down to dinner, as the guest, I was asked to give thanks, I did. My daddy said that when eating at my grandmother's house, my grandfather always gave thanks before each meal. He talked about my grandfather's sopping dessert. This got a laugh all around.

The meal was delicious, and the apple pie dessert was very special. Helga, my grandmother, baked it and still did occasionally bake for neighbors when paid to do so.

The evening was very enjoyable, and I felt at ease and welcomed. We all sat around and talked for a while after the meal. My daddy talked about his father, my grandfather, and about him being a shoe cobbler. He found out when he came back to Germany that his father had been forced to repair leather items for the Nazis during the war, items such as motorcycle saddle bags, combat boots, and rifle slings. He said he only saw his father a few times when he came back before he was killed by the wall that fell on him. He then showed me a picture taken just four days before he died. I again could see the resemblance that I had to him, my grandfather, as I had when I first saw Hans.

I asked if they had a camera so that pictures could be made because I wanted to send Mama one. Grettle got her camera and made several pictures of all of us and then I took the camera and made pictures of them.

As I got ready to leave, Helga, my grandmother, came over and gave me a very clinging hug. We all agreed that we would get together again in a month at the farm.

141

During the next thirty days, I wrote a couple of letters to Mama, bringing her up to date about what had transpired and promised to send pictures that I would later get from Grettle. I didn't know if by now she had told my stepfather about this whole story or not.

Duty at ACA was routine, but since I had been assigned there two other GIs, Burley Champion and Mark Bruther, had been shipped out to Vietnam and replaced by Carl Parrott and Ned Baird. I knew that was probably going to be my fate when my tour here in Berlin was over.

At 4:30 P.M. the next day, while on post at the front entrance, I watched the vehicles of the British, French, and Americans come out and their replacements come in. Movement was slow due to heavy construction traffic on the street. They all had the usual occupants, a sergeant driver, a lieutenant, and either a colonel or lieutenant colonel. Afterwards, the Russian replacement shift came in, and those being replaced were the last to emerge. This was a little unusual; they were most often the first relief shift to arrive and the first end of shift to depart.

Just as the car got clear of the front gate, no more than forty feet away, it was hit head-on by a large dump truck carrying concrete debris from the nearby construction site. It was a horrendous wreck. The car was demolished, and the truck had severe damage.

Immediately, two of my coworkers came outside the building upon hearing the noise of the wreck. I could not leave my post until my relief was on site but one of my coworkers was my relief who was due to take over in thirty minutes. I outranked him, and I instructed him to take over my post so I could try to help those injured. At that moment a German man, a neighbor who lived in an apartment across the street, came outside, saw the carnage and yelled that he was going to call the police and ambulance.

The only thing I could do was put a tourniquet around the lieutenant's leg and help him and the sergeant out of the vehicle. The colonel, who was in the back seat, got out of the vehicle on his own and immediately passed out on the sidewalk. The noise of the sirens was deafening, there were three ambulances and two German police cars on site within minutes. The colonel was put into an ambulance by himself. The driver looked familiar; it was Gerhard, my uncle. The lieutenant and sergeant were both put in one ambulance and the truck driver another. The police directed traffic and assisted the wreckers in removing the two vehicles. I learned later that the Russians dispatched a wrecker to pick up their car and an East Berlin ambulance to get the sergeant and lieutenant. No word was forthcoming about the colonel.

The next week, we all got together at the farm. This time, Gerhard and my grandmother, picked me up in the car at ACA and we drove to the farm in Pertz. I asked where Grettle was, Gerhard said she was doing her duty as a nurse trying to take care of an important person. It was a Saturday, and the plan was that we would stay overnight and return to Berlin early Sunday. The ride down was overwhelming with the odor of delicious pie that Grandmother had made to carry along with us. I kiddingly suggested halfway there that we stop and have a picnic with the main and only course being pie. All laughed but did not go along with the suggestion.

We arrived with Daddy meeting us at the front porch. We all had lightweight overnight luggage that we brought inside and put in respective bedrooms. Aunt Grettle surprised me as she came out of a room that I had not been into before. She asked me and Gerhard to come into the room. When I walked in, I saw the Russian, Colonel Drowbeski sitting in a chair. He had a bandage on his head and one arm in a sling. I was very surprised and concerned at what I saw. I asked Gerhard what was going on here. He said that he and Grettle were working with Captain Currin and the "Agency." He then said I think that you recognized me when Grettle, I, and Helga first came here to the farm to meet you several months ago, and of course I recognized you. He said that Colonel Drowbeski was defecting to the US and that a car would be here at any moment to pick him up. He was in danger as the Russians were looking everywhere for him. The colonel then spoke up saying it disgusted him, the shooting and killing people who were trying to cross from East to West Berlin. All they wanted was freedom and, in some cases, just to be with their families. He said he had been working at ACA for eighteen months and crossing into West from the East you could see the contrast. He saw this on a daily basis, how the economy was so different, and you could see that the people were mostly happy and content. He said he had been providing information to the US via the litter thrown from the car. He knew he was now under suspicion, so he had to get out before he was put under a firing squad. I asked, isn't everything at ACA an open book to all that work there, and he answered yes, then said the information he was providing was about other things he was privy to. Gerhard said this whole operation was set up by the "Agency," the only problem was the truck crashing into the car was more damaging than planned. He then explained that Grettle had come here with the colonel immediately after the "accident." As a retired nurse, she was able to care for the colonel's injuries. I asked how Daddy and Grandmother felt about all this and was it putting them and us in danger. They were all right with it and because of all the precautions, he didn't think any of us were in danger.

At that moment, a car was heard driving up outside and then there was a knock on the door. Grettle went out to answer it. Two men came into the house and two remained outside with the car. They escorted Colonel Drowbeski out into the car and quickly drove away.

The weather was beautiful, so we went for a walk around the farm to relieve the tension. There was a new calf Daddy wanted us all to see and a horse he had recently bought. As we were walking, a neighbor drove up and came out to join us. As he was walking toward us from his truck, Daddy said that he was a good friend that helped here on the farm when help was needed. He said all of his family already knew this man. When he got to us, Daddy introduced him to me.

His name was Werner Tobler. We shook hands and then the realization hit me, this was the other POW that had worked on my granddaddy's farm. This was just amazing to me that Corporal Werner Tobler and my daddy, Sergeant Hans Krause had remained close friends all these years and saw each other weekly.

After the walk we all returned to the house where Grettle and Grandmother put together a delicious meal. We were joined by Werner who had been told about me after my first visit by Daddy. Werner said he had grown up in Pertz, and his family had always known Daddy's uncle and aunt that had previously owned the farm. He had never met Hans until they were assigned to work together as sniper and spotter on the Russian front. They could hardly believe that they had so much in common. Daddy said that there were so many unbelievable coincidences in "our whole story" that the odds of all that had occurred was just amazing. Werner said he had two grown children that grew up in Pertz with he and his wife, who passed away five years ago. He said that Daddy and he even had that in common, both losing their wives five years ago. They both had given each other support then and all the way back to 1943.

Werner wanted to know all about my grandparents, Uncle Brindell, and the farm. Daddy had already told him about my "other" Daddy and Mama.

After the delicious pie dessert, Werner left to head home and we all went to bed, with Daddy and I sharing a bed.

The next morning, we had breakfast, talked a lot, then had a light lunch. Afterwards we said our goodbyes and drove back to Berlin where Gerhard dropped me off at the front entrance to ACA. Just before I got out of the car, Grettle gave me copies of pictures, two with Daddy and I, two with all of them that I took, and two with all of them with me. Grettle took the picture so of course she wasn't in it. I forwarded a copy to Mama.

On the next day that I had off, I intended to keep the promise that I had made to Betsy Ann Moyer, the lady at the office of Military Data pre-1948 at the Berlin Capital Building. She had made me promise to come back to tell her about meeting my real daddy. She brought me into her office and closed the door, gave me a seat, and said start from the beginning. I told her the whole story about the Double A Whistler sniper shooting the Nazi sniper, about him winding up on the farm of the American that shot him, and all the rest of it. Even the part about Corporal Tobler being from Pertz and knowing Daddy's uncle and aunt and that they are best friends now.

She was amazed and intrigued. She said this is like something you would read about in a book and suggested I write about it. She wanted to know how I was treated by my daddy and his family. I brought pictures to show her, and she smiled and wiped away a couple of tears.

The next day, I was summoned to Brigade Headquarters for a closed meeting with Captain Currin and again the man in civilian clothes. It was a debriefing of the events regarding the wreck at the front entrance, the defection of the colonel and the involvement of my family members, here in Berlin and the farm in Pertz. The man in civvies warned me, "ordered" me not to talk to anyone about what had happened. He then said it was almost unbelievable the co-incidences in this situation. I told him this was only a small portion of the whole story of coinci-dences. He asked me what I meant, and I told him all of it. He and the captain said it was hard to believe and just shook their heads.

My tour of duty in Berlin was coming to an end in six weeks, and I had been given orders to travel back to the US for special training at Fort

Monmouth, New Jersey. Once completed I would go to Fort Sam Houston, Texas for three months and then to Vietnam.

By now, I had mastered the German phone system, so I called Daddy and gave him the news. He was upset about it; I could hear it in his voice. He wanted us all to get together again before I shipped out. He said he would make some plans and I should get back to him to see if they fit my work schedule. He asked me to call him back in three days.

When I called him, he asked when I had the next weekend off. I told him it was the weekend before I shipped out on a Wednesday. He said he would like for us all to be his guest at the farm again and Gerhard and family would pick me up at ACA and drive down as before; I agreed.

On my last Friday in Berlin, they picked me up at ACA, and we drove to the farm. The mood this time was more somber, but the wonderful odor of baked pie was just as good as before. Grettle and Grandmother kept asking when I might be coming back to Berlin or the farm. I didn't know and told them that I certainly

151

wanted to, but at present I had no way of knowing. When we got to the farm, Daddy and Werner were there waiting. Daddy had already prepared a lavish meal, which was enjoyed by all. I said to my grandmother that one of the greatest incentives for my return were her pies. She said if I did, she would make me a different one every day. After dessert, Werner shook my hand, said it was a pleasure to know his friend Hans finally had an heir and that he hoped to see me again. I didn't think too much about his words, but said I was glad to have met him and that you never know, I may be back soon.

The next day after breakfast, we all rode into town. We went to church, then visited my granddaddy's grave. My grandmother had brought along flowers to place on it. Next, we walked around town and had lunch at a small restaurant. Afterwards we went back to the farm where my daddy and I went out to check on the new calf and other animals. After feeding, them he asked me how I would like to live here. I told him it seemed to be a very nice place to live. His next words caught me off guard. He said one day this will all be yours. I asked what he meant. He said you are my only heir and the farm will be left to you when I'm gone. I started to speak but he stopped me. He said I know you may never live here; I know you may sell it, but it is going to be yours to do with as you want. It was really hard to believe this, but he was very sincere and re-assured me that he meant every word. He said he had talked to his mother and sister, and they had no objection since it was his and he had lived there and worked it; he could do with it what he wanted to. Walking back to the house, I was somewhat speechless, trying to take it all in.

The evening meal prepared by Aunt Grettle and Grandmother was delicious as usual but the highlight was again the pie, this time blueberry with vanilla ice cream on top. I told Grand-mother that if I kept eating her pie, I would not be able to fit into my clothes. She understood, laughed and said she could also sew and do al-terations.

The after-meal talk tonight was somewhat muted with the dread of tomorrow's goodbyes.

The next morning breakfast was quick, and we

put our few thing's into the car for the trip back to Berlin.

Daddy asked me to come into the kitchen where the table was. We sat down and he pulled an envelope out of his shirt pocket and opened it. He pulled out the 1785 coin that I had just returned to him a few months earlier.

He said, "I want you to take this with you; remember it belonged to your great-great-great-grandfather. It is a good luck piece; it saved my father's life, your grandfather in World War I. He was in one of the trenches in France. It was quiet, early that day on the battlefront. Everyone's nerves were on edge, expecting either the whistle to be blown, signaling for them to attack or the sound of incoming artillery rounds.

"To ease the tension and occupy their minds with more distant thoughts, he and his buddy started flipping coins, calling heads or tails. They were not gambling, just passing the time, guessing, heads or tails. He had the 1785 coin given to him by his father, my grandfather, who had told him it was a good luck coin. He didn't believe or disbelieve that, but to honor his father's wishes he took it. He promised he would keep it and bring it back to him, when he returned from the war.

"As he flipped the coin into the air an enemy artillery shell exploded nearby. He was stunned and the concussion knocked him off his feet. He was not injured, but the coin was lost. The whistle to attack was blown and the platoon, all except he, climbed out of the trench, to engage the enemy. He lingered behind, searching in the bottom of the trench for the coin he had promised to bring back to his father, your great grandfather. At that moment his whole platoon was wiped out with a barrage of artillery shells. They were out of the trench, exposed above ground while he was on his hands and knees looking for the coin in the bottom of the trench. In the midst, of the carnage he found the coin and put it in his pocket. He returned it to his father three months later at the end of the war.

"It did save his life in a most unusual way. He only told what happened once, to his father. He never put much belief in it being a 'good luck coin' because all of his platoon members were killed, and he felt guilty because he was the only survivor. I only knew this story because my grandfather told it to me when he gave me the coin, when I became a Nazi soldier. He died two months later, and my father never talked about the coin.

"You know now why it is a good luck coin. It has been passed down in the family through several generations. It saved my life in World War II, it cared well for me, brought love to me and a son." As he said those words, tears fell onto the coin just as they did when Mama held it in the hayloft in 1946. He said, "I'm sure it will keep you safe in Vietnam and when you come back here, bring it with you."

We went out to the porch to say our good-byes. He hugged me and said, "I love you my son, be safe."

I returned the hug and said, "Goodbye, Daddy." My thoughts immediately went back to January 1957. The only time I ever said goodbye to my daddy Wilson, I never saw him alive again.